About the Author

Born to a middle class family in Karachi, Pakistan, I had an educated and loving upbringing.

I saw first-hand the growth of the Taliban in my city, Karachi. In fact, I was approached by them to join their mujahedeen cause. I encountered deaths of innocent civilians from suicide bombing by the Taliban and other Islamic extremist groups. These experiences, alongside my scientific and philosophical curiosity, turned me into an agnostic.

I decided to write this book in hope of bringing an understanding to the reader about the choices that some of us faced during the rise of Taliban in Pakistan.

Paradise Without Virgins

Ash

Paradise Without Virgins

Olympia Publishers
London

www.olympiapublishers.com
OLYMPIA PAPERBACK EDITION

Copyright © Ash 2020

The right of Ash to be identified as author of
this work has been asserted in accordance with sections 77 and 78
of the Copyright, Designs and Patents Act 1988.

All Rights Reserved

No reproduction, copy or transmission of this publication
may be made without written permission.
No paragraph of this publication may be reproduced,
copied or transmitted save with the written permission of the
publisher, or in accordance with the provisions
of the Copyright Act 1956 (as amended).

Any person who commits any unauthorised act in relation to
this publication may be liable to criminal
prosecution and civil claims for damage.

A CIP catalogue record for this title is
available from the British Library.

ISBN: 978-1-78830-594-5

This is a work of fiction.
Names, characters, places and incidents originate from the writer's
imagination. Any resemblance to actual persons, living or dead, is
purely coincidental.

First Published in 2020

Olympia Publishers
Tallis House
2 Tallis Street
London
EC4Y 0AB
Printed in Great Britain

Dedication

To all those loving souls who lost their lives because of religious extremism

Acknowledgements

My family, friends and my dog for their unwavering love and support

1

Abu Bakr Mosque Karachi, Pakistan, year 2000.

"You must help your brothers fighting in Kashmir — Prophet Muhammad said, 'the war of one Muslim against oppression is the war of all the Muslims around the world'. Your sisters! Your mothers! They are being raped all over in Kashmir, Palestine and many other places but what are you doing about it? Nothing! Absolutely nothing!

"Just imagine for a minute, my brothers; if an Indian soldier storms into your house here in Karachi, puts his gun to your head, ties you down and rapes your sister, your mother, your daughter or your wife in front of your eyes — what will you do then?! Will you not fight him? Kill him with your own hands? Or die as a martyr protecting their dignity and your honour? I know you would. Because if you would not, then I say you are a coward and cowards are not worthy of paradise! Instead, they will rot in hell along with the oppressors!

"Remember my brothers — we Muslims are brothers and sisters to one another. Therefore, the rape of a Muslim woman in Kashmir or anywhere else means your own sister, your wife, your daughter, your mother has been raped! Isn't that true? Tell me my brothers isn't it?"

Uthman, a mujahid (fighter) from Jaish-e-Mohammad ('The Army of Muhammad'), an Islamic militant group having close ties with the Taliban, both in Afghanistan and Pakistan, is articulate. He needs to be, as his task is a difficult one; it demands him to convince the young Muslims from every corner, every household, to join the mujahidin in their fight against India to liberate Kashmir.

He is especially on a look out for youth of lower uneducated labour class. Their vulnerability lies in not being able to secure any meaningful education or a source of income to lead sufficient lifestyles. So they pass their days mostly with a degree of lack of ambition to make any worldly gains. Instead, they wish for all the luxuries to be granted to them by Allah in paradise and put all their focus on doing deeds here that would benefit them in the life here after. Jihad for Allah is one of them; in fact, sacrificing one's own life for him and his cause is the pinnacle of jihad, guaranteeing paradise and its seventy-two virgins.

Convincing such youth to join the mujahidin cause and getting them to believe in it is an art that Uthman has mastered over time. His command over words of the local languages, his godly demeanour, combined with his good looks — deep green eyes and fair skin, taken as a sign of nobility by many regressive Muslims in Pakistan — has made him the top recruiter of jihadists, not just in Karachi but from all over Pakistan.

Before joining 'The Army of Muhammad' and moving to Pakistan, Uthman spent his early years being a member of the US-funded al-Qaeda in Afghanistan to fight against the Soviets. Once the cold war ended, he continued working for Osama bin Laden but this time fighting against the Americans. With an established reputation of a top recruiter, he was approached by the leaders of the newly formed 'The Army of

Muhammad', to assist them in recruiting new jihadists. With the blessings of al-Qaeda chiefs, he agreed to join 'The Army of Muhammad', an organization that is not only recognized by al-Qaeda but is also fully supported by them both financially and, in terms of providing supreme leadership and direction by Osama bin Laden.

Uthman silences the mumbling in the crowd by continuing in a firm and logical voice. "Like it or not, my brothers, these are your sisters that are being raped by the Indians in Kashmir. These are your brothers who are dying every day trying to protect their honour. So if there runs in you the blood of a true Muslim, blood of a true soldier of Allah, then what is stopping you to leave whatever you are doing right now and join me to liberate our Muslim brothers and sisters living in Kashmir from the Kafir Indians? Ask yourself, my able-bodied men, since when did you become caught up in chasing the bounty for this ephemeral life when you should be amassing the bounties of the eternal life here after? What better way to guarantee yourself, your family and your future generations a place in Jannah, other than jihad in the name of Allah? And guarantee yourselves a place in paradise."

Abu Bakar Mosque is in the heart of the city of Karachi. It is a minimalistic structure made of cemented walls bearing white paint and a green dome. Mounted on the dome is a bronze-plated replica representing a half-moon. The majority of the worshippers attending the mosque belong to the working class. The mosque is state funded but also receives generous donations from some of its more wealthy worshippers. The mosque's walls are fifty-foot-high and the wide rows, thirty in total, are laid opposite to the rostrum with perfect precision, going all the way back to the veranda. The first row is highly privileged and sought after as in any other mosque, as the Muslim worshippers believe that here, the blessings received from the prayers are multiplied in numbers. So, it is filled mostly with eager old men who have either arrived very early or are allowed to move ahead by the young worshippers out of respect.

Friday afternoon prayers, or Jema'ah prayers, brings the largest crowd of worshippers to every mosque, including the Abu Bakar Mosque, compared to any other prayer during the week. This is because both the Quran and the Prophet Muhammad declared Jema'ah prayers as more bountiful than other weekly prayers. Hence people from every walk of life flock their way to the mosque on this day. This provides a big hunting ground for the likes of Uthman, therefore he has earlier requested the Imam of Abu Bakr Mosque to grant him five minutes to deliver a short recruitment speech before the Imam begins the Jema'ah sermon. The Imam himself is a supporter of Islamic radicalization and believes that no other form of government should prevail in the universe except for the one that promotes Sharia law. So he has happily granted Uthman the five minutes he needs to deliver his message.

Fit for the occasion, Uthman is neatly draped in a clean, wrinkle-free white kandura which is an ankle-length garment with long sleeves. His fair skin appears to be whiter than any other object inside the mosque. His brown beard, that matches his iris, reflects streaks of red when the rays of hot October sun falls on it. He stands tall on the rostrum with an AK 47 hanging from his left shoulder and continues to address the mass with an arrogance that gives the impression, as if Allah himself speaks through his voice. "Believe me, my brothers — Allah has held my hand and he will hold the hands of all the comrades that will be serving 'The Army of Muhammad'. So do not hesitate and swear allegiance to me. Together we will grow t 'The Army of Muhammad', blessed by Allah and his beloved Prophet. And instead, if you choose to go back to your homes from here by giving a deaf ear towards the call of your dying Muslim brothers and sisters in Kashmir, then ask yourself — will you ever be able to find peace in your hearts? Would you be able to sleep with a clear conscience at night? Is it worth to trade the eternal heaven with the temporary comfort of your beds in this meaningless world?"

Uthman pierces his gaze through the front rows, purposely ignoring the old men in front. He thinks that these timeworn men have committed many sins in their lives and just as now their penises can no longer satisfy their lusts and have their feet hanging in their graves, they are begging Allah for forgiveness! Youth is what Uthman is interested in, so his gaze finally rests upon two physically fit boys, about seventeen to eighteen years old — Siddiq and Adnan. The boys appear to be confused; Uthman's carefully crafted words have penetrated through their minds and into their conscience.

Sensing that he has reached a point where the deep water meets the shallow water and he is about to catch some fish, Uthman raises his voice and continues. "So, join me, my able-bodied brothers, so that you are able to justify all the health and strength given to you by Allah. Those fathers among you who are too old to join — encourage your sons to join instead. You and your sons will not only have Allah's mercy in this world but you will achieve greatness by joining the prophets and the nobles in the afterlife. I and my comrades are here for only two more days, so hurry up and don't let this opportunity go by. Don't forget that you will be answerable to Allah on the day of judgement. Stood in front of the Almighty, you will be asked as to what you did when I came to you requesting you to join his army — what answer will you give him then? That you chose the comfort of your temporary lives while your Muslim brothers and sisters suffered? Come and see us, my brothers. We will guide you and teach you all you need to know. We will look after you, feed you and even give you extra money to send back home to your families. And if for any reason you or your sons cannot join, then at least donate as much as possible today and buy yourself a place in Jannah! Peace be upon you."

He steps down from the rostrum, looking up to the heavens, and hands the microphone over to the Imam who, moved by Uthman's soul-searching speech, decides to deliver his Friday sermon around the importance of jihad.

"All praise is to Allah, the most beneficial and the merciful. Today, our brother Uthman has touched our spirits by his honest account of the problems faced by the Muslim brothers all over the world; I encourage you to whole heartedly support him in his cause…"

Siddiq and Adnan could not pay attention to what the Imam is saying any more. Their minds are still captivated by Uthman's words and his saintly aura. They feel, with different intensities, that they cannot simply ignore what Uthman has just said and carry on with their lives. This is exactly what Uthman is famous for — impregnating young hearts with seeds of self-doubt and making them question their way of life, so they carry strong guilt of having abandoned their brothers and sisters in Kashmir if they decide not to join the mujahidin. The feeling can quickly shift from one of guilt to the one of fear that Allah will punish them, both here in this world and in hell if they turned their back on jihad and chose to stay back for their worldly life. So eventually, many youngsters have turned to Uthman as they could no longer deal with these ill feelings of self-doubt and wanted to attain peace within themselves.

However, some have also turned to Uthman not because of any guilt or fear, but instead they possess a genuine desire to meet their Almighty Allah. Those are the ones who are willing to die for their Allah, more than they are willing to live for themselves or for its subjects on earth. Much easier to manage by the mujahidin compared to the indecisive ones who need more persuasion. However, indecisiveness among some youth is perceived as vulnerability that Uthman and his men have exploited successfully in the past. They have greeted such young men with open arms, assuring them that they are doing right by Allah, their creator, and promising them that their souls will be liberated, and paradise is guaranteed to them. Uthman and the mujahidin have also truly believed that salvation is possible only through jihad. So, whenever they have opened their arms for such young recruits, they have been able to do that with honesty, which is readily felt by the recruits.

Siddiq and Adnan feel the same vulnerability; they also feel that on the other hand, if they do join Uthman in his 'Army of Muhammad' then they risk their lives. Not only that but also, they have to leave behind everything that they hold dear, and fight the enemy which now suddenly feels their own! The fear of dying alone, even though as a martyr, is strong enough in Siddiq's mind for deciding against joining the 'Army of Muhammad'. But, almost immediately, the fear is replaced by the guilt of abandoning his comrades on this sacred mission. These strong feelings of guilt and fear have made him very uneasy.

Both the boys are camped inside the mosque for I'tikāf; a practice in which believers retreat in the mosque for the last ten days of Ramadan, ensuring that they spend 'Laylat Al-Qadr' (the night during which they believe Allah forgives all sins) in the act of worship. Siddiq and Adnan belong to the lower middle-class religious families who do not agree with Islamic radicalization in principle. However, they do not disagree with it strongly enough either, to have ever raised their voice against radicalization outside their own four walls. Financially, there is not much difference between their families but Siddiq's family is relatively more educated than Adnan's with Siddiq's parents having sound jobs in a local bank. Siddiq has been brought up in a studious environment where both his elder sisters being doctors and where he himself aspires to become a computer software engineer. He hasn't got much in common intellectually with Adnan but they always spend the late afternoons playing cricket together with other boys in their neighbourhood street. So, when it was time to decide which camp Siddiq will pick during his stay in the mosque for the last ten days of holy month of Ramadan, next to Adnan's camp was his obvious choice. In fact, Adnan played a strong part in convincing Siddiq to sit for I'tikāf in the first place. He pointed out to Siddiq that because Siddiq does not attend the mosque five times a day each day, staying in the mosque for the last ten days of the holy month to busy himself with prayers to Allah only, would make up for all the prior slack on his behalf.

"What do you think about the speech he just delivered?" Siddiq mumbles to Adnan while keeping his gaze towards the Imam.

Adnan, being in a similar state of confusion as per Siddiq, replies with a whisper, "I don't know but I cannot ignore what he has just said and carry on with my daily life! The weight of his words has pressed hard against my conscience. I'll need to do something — I don't know — let's talk about it after the prayers."

Siddiq nods his head in agreement. In the meantime, the Imam steps down from the rostrum, turns his back towards the worshippers and faces towards the Qibla — the direction that should be faced when performing the prayer. He then asks the worshippers to stand in straight rows behind him. Within seconds, worshippers organize themselves in straight rows with adults in the centre and children being at both ends of each row. The Imam then calls out, "Allah ho Akbar"— the prayers have now begun.

2

Layla almost died of excessive bleeding during her Caesarean section, but that didn't bother her, as after three girls, the Ansari family is finally blessed with a baby boy. Even though times have changed significantly from the days when some Arab men used to bury their daughters alive but still, a boy's birth is celebrated more compared to a girl in majority of the Pakistani households. In case of the Ansari family, this baby boy will be the first to carry the family name forwards. Layla feels that Allah has opened the gates of heaven for her as the boy arrived in the holy month of Ramadan. What's more, the boy also looks like a mullah — like a mini version of Bin Laden — with a long face and tiny, but visible, facial hair that one might safely call a beard.

Layla is a liberal woman but at the same time likes to maintain her spiritual connection with Allah. She reads books on Sufism (an off-shoot of liberal Islam with roots connected to Turkey and the famous philosopher Rumi) and believes that her relationship with the divine is one that of a friend. She feels that she doesn't need to pray five times a day to seek the Lord's blessings. She is sure that Allah communicates with her through her feelings and sometimes give her divine signals whenever she needs any help or direction especially when she is confronted with any problem

Layla was raised by her uncle, who she lovingly calls Baba. A PhD in Politics from UC Berkeley — a man of vision who she adored the most but let him down when she married Omar.

'Baba was right about Omar', she thinks...

'Didn't he prove himself to be a narrow-minded religious wanker? A typical Pakistani male chauvinist! Suppressing my ambitions and my views! How each time he kicked up a fuss when I got dressed to attend a gathering of The Karachi Writers Association! Accusing me of mixing shamelessly with loose men who smoked hashish and sipped wine! I was so naive at that time that I shared my every experience with him, thinking of him as a friend, just like Baba was to his wife. But clearly, Omar was never the type. He exploited my honesty by using the experiences I shared with him and tried to bring me down whenever he wished! I felt bullied, because of his controlled and passive-aggressive actions and taunts. And if that wasn't enough, he went as far as suspecting me of having an affair with God knows who!

I wonder what it would've been like to have an affair with those writers who gave me so much attention. Some even had the courage to come up to me and ask me out even though they knew I was married! I wore my wedding band all the time! Some just watched from a distance like hungry predators — scanning every curve of my body through my fine Indian silk saris. It wouldn't surprise me if they imagined me naked and held onto the image until they had gone home to bed their wives and cum inside them picturing me in their heads. Imagine if anyone of them had accidently cried out my name during orgasm? Poor fellow would've been thrown out of the house by his wife, surely?'

It had brought a cheeky smile to Layla eyes, imagining those men begging their angry wives for forgiveness. She then consoles herself by looking at the boy and saying, "Nevertheless, Omar provides for all of us and he is a good man, a good father. But I want you to be like Baba when you grow up, my little one. Strong, liberal, honest and respecting women. Plus, you are so beautiful, my baby boy! I know all the girls will be chasing after you!"

She waits for Omar to come and pick them up from the Civil Services Hospital, Karachi. It has just gone past nine a.m. He has dropped their daughter Hafsa at the nearby nursery and then making his way to the hospital which is only a ten-minute drive from the nursery. Layla hasn't packed her and the baby's stuff — that is for Omar to sort out. Layla has made it clear to him that he shouldn't expect her to do any house chores for at least a month post the delivery, as, after all, dealing with the burden of pregnancy for nine months, she needs her time to relax and wants to be pampered alongside the baby.

There is a knock, on Layla's hospital room door.

"Surely this can't be Omar — knocking is beyond his mannerism!" she murmurs, and then follows it up with a low pitch but loud enough 'yes', so as not to wake the baby up. The door opens and the nurse, who looks no more than twenty-five years old, enters the room with the breakfast trolley. She has silky, black hair, wearing sparkling clean but slightly wrinkled uniform that is fitted tightly around her tall skinny body and her name badge pinned to her uniform.

"Good morning, ma'am. Scrambled egg on toast with butter, chocolate chip muffin, fruits and coffee — exactly how you asked for yesterday." The nurse begins to pull out the contents of the trolley and places them on the table next to the bed with a glowing smile on her face. She asks Layla, "How is the little bundle of joy this morning?"

Layla replies with a pause, "Very well! Thank you." She wants to ask the nurse how is she doing but instead gets distracted by the huge love bite that becomes visible on the side of her neck as her hair swerves down towards the floor, while she puts the breakfast on the table.

Clearing her throat, she says to the nurse, while trying to give her an eye contact "Seems like somebody had an exciting night!" she catches the nurse off guard.

"I'm sorry, ma'am, I didn't catch that," the nurse replies hurriedly, wondering how this woman, who has just given birth and is only agile enough to leave her bed when nature calls, could possibly know what she has been up to during the night with the senior doctor on duty!

'No one saw us! It's impossible! We made out in the doctor's office — how the hell does this lazy cow know'? The nurse's mind starts to panic and her heart races. She doesn't give Layla any eye contact and hastily goes about her business to walk out from the room as quick as she can.

Layla, sees that she has made the nurse conscious about her appearance, so instead of labouring on the topic she says, "Thank you for the breakfast!" then picks up an orange and starts peeling it, giving the nurse an opportunity to gather herself.

The nurse composes herself. "You are welcome, ma'am!" Then hurries out of the room without having another look towards Layla or the baby.

Layla then looks at the door behind her and whispers, "Poor little girl, I made her uncomfortable. When was the last time Omar and I made out passionately like this girl and whoever her lover was?" She takes the seeds out of her slice of orange and begins to eat.

The door opens without a knock this time, within moments of the nurse leaving the room. Omar, Layla's husband, arrives with an anxious look on his face and walks straight towards their boy who is asleep in the cot and whispers, "Salaam, my little one! My boy! My life!" He then sits next to Layla on the bed with a worried look on his face and asks, "Did you guys sleep well?" but without giving Layla any time to reply, he continues… "The Anti-Shiite Green Turbans have shot dead Dr. Zaidi last night."

Layla almost choked on her orange juice. "What? How? Omar, are you serious?" *(The green turban is a term used locally to refer to a banned extremist religious group of Sipah-e-Sahaba who believe that Shiites are heretics who call themselves Muslims and that they should be eradicated from Pakistan and from the world. They condemn Shiite to be blasphemous as Shiite's acknowledge Ali, the nephew and son-in-law of Prophet Muhammad, to be the righteous caliph after Prophet's death. So, for Sipah-e-Sahaba killing a Shiite is a way to guarantee them a place in Paradise.)*

Omar continues, "They say Dr. Zaidi was constantly receiving death threats from the Sipah-e-Sahaba[3] wanting him to shut his clinic down within fifteen days, that is by the middle of Ramadan, and never to show his Shiite face in Orangi Town again." In complete horror Layla keeps her light brown eyes fixed at Omar as he continues, "At first, Dr. Zaidi refused, saying that he has the clinic in Orangi Town for the last fifteen years, all the patients know him and he is a family doctor to many; plus it is his and his family's bread and butter so he cannot just leave! But then he realized that this was serious, as the Sipah-e-Sahaba activists began firing shots in the air at the doorstep of his clinic from time to time. He then agreed to leave the town but told them that he will need at least three months to find himself a new place elsewhere. They went quiet for a bit — Dr. Zaidi thought that they have agreed to it. They didn't buy that, Layla — so last night, on the twenty-first day of Ramadan, they send one of his own patients to kill him! A green turban motherfucker whose ear infection Dr. Zaidi cured recently, they say. That bastard shot him in the neck! Dr. Zaidi tried to drive himself to the hospital but collapsed on the wheel — couldn't even make it out of the garage!"

"Where were his staff?" Layla finally finds her voice back.

"They went home — it was after hours," Omar replies, with his face pointing down towards the floor, distinctive wavy lines running across his forehead showing signs of empathy and grave sadness in his eyes.

"His children, Kashif and Zainab, are so young and his poor wife, Madiha, didn't she have enough problems with her health already? She has never even worked in her life — how will she manage with two kids? I feel so bad for her!" Layla expects Omar to respond but this time Omar is lost for words, his eyes turning red with anger and sorrow.

Still keeping his gaze towards the floor and with a sombre voice, Omar tells Layla, "The funeral is tonight — I don't expect you to be there; in fact, I'd rather you are not be there — you've just come out of this difficult pregnancy, of course. But I will go and I'll probably take Dad along with me."

Without hesitating, Layla grabs Omar by his wrists and says like she means it, "No! Please don't go to the funeral, Omar! It is dangerous! You could just go to their house to offer our condolences and that should be enough. No way am I going to let you and Dad go to the Imam Bargah *(Shiite term for a mosque)* for the funeral. You know very well that when they strike once, they then strike again. It is very risky; these sister-fucker Sipah-e-Sahaba, bloody allies of Taliban, do not even think twice before blowing themselves up for that disgusting promise of seventy-two virgins! Their God is a fucking sex-crazed callous maniac! I cannot understand what sorts of mothers give birth to these mindless barbarians!" The anger in Layla's voice suddenly changes into something more fearful, "I beg you, Omar, please don't go! I fear that they will target the funeral to kill more Shiites."

Omar can immediately feel the fear that Layla was able to raise inside him. He knows that what Layla has just said could well be true and there is a real chance that the Sipah-e-Sahaba might strike twice and attempt to bomb the funeral proceedings.

Omar finally turns to Layla and consoles her. "The path to heaven that these Sipah-e-Sahaba members have constructed in their minds is disgusting. You are right, my love, they won't think twice before blowing themselves up again, may it be at the funeral if they get an opportunity. OK, mother of my children — I'll visit Madiha and family at their home. You are right; it is probably safer not to attend the funeral."

He then turns his attention at the little boy who is still sleeping. "My little gift from heaven is right here — what more could I want? We should start making our way home now; Mom and Dad must be waiting for you two at home. Mom was preparing breakfast when I left this morning. It must be a feast! Can't wait!"

Omar, having done this several times before for Layla, packs all her stuff swiftly and within the next twenty minutes they leave the room with the smell of the un-touched croissant that the nurse has brought earlier.

3

Adnan is enrolled in a local community science college but hardly shows up for any lectures. In fact, he proudly recalls to his friends that he has been to the college only twice in his first year; once at the enrolment day and then when the college handed out the examination admission cards. However, because of his extremely amicable personality and kind heartedness, Adnan makes friends instantly. He is well known among his neighbourhood for his gentle demeanour and is often found taking the blind man living two blocks away from his apartment to the mosque.

Adnan's father runs a small business of gas appliances which he visits in the evenings to help his father out. Adnan's brother is trying to adjust to his new career in real estate after losing money, most of which were his client's, in the Karachi Stock Exchange. For the majority of the time his clients were after him — threatening to break his bones if he is unable to return their money. His life was spared only because his mother sold all her gold jewellery so that he was able to pay off some of the debts to the ones that threatened him the most. Finally, like most of the women in the neighbourhood, Adnan's mother is a devoted housewife. Her sense of duty towards her husband and her two sons is unwavering. She hardly ever falls sick, never fails to cook three fresh meals each day for her family and prays five times a day to Allah for their welfare. She believes that she is truly blessed, her sons never lie to her nor do they commit any vile sins, and for the sins that they do commit, they are stemmed from naivety rather than malice. Like his mother, Adnan consoles himself about the lack of money, facilities and fun in his life by thinking about Allah and the life hereafter. He believes that being a good Muslim is more crucial than to have a career or to be good at sports because the real test will be on the Day of Judgement. It is clear to him that if he comes out as a winner in front of Allah on the Day of Judgment, he will have the best life for eternity.

For Siddiq, remembering the prayers by heart comes in handy, as his focus is still on the words spoken by Uthman while the Imam leads the prayers. He also feels that his friend Adnan, being more decisive and pushy towards doing right by Allah, will somehow be able to convince him to join 'The Army of Muhammad', just like he was able to convince him to sit for I'tikāf with him. To Siddiq, it is obvious that Adnan will join Uthman and his 'Army of Muhammad'.

He recalls Adnan's words that he spoke with certainty to him two nights ago on the veranda of the mosque when they both sat talking after night prayers. 'Siddiq, I do many things for my parents, my friends, my neighbours and I get their love in return. Allah loves me more than my parents, my friends, more than anyone, but I don't think I do enough for him. I'm sure he wants something from me — I must have a purpose to fulfil. I hope one day he sends me a clear sign wanting me to do something for him. Since I love him the most, I talk to him the most and want to be with him the most, I'll do whatever he asks of me, Siddiq. I don't know what opportunity Allah will give me to serve him but I know that he will — he gives it to all his pupils who believe in him. I just don't want to disappoint him, because if I do then he will abandon me. I'll be alone and totally lost. I pray to him every day that he gives me strength to serve him well'.

So this is most definitely the opportunity that Adnan has been craving for, surely, Siddiq thinks to himself, dragging his focus back on the Friday prayers.

Siddiq is not ready to die. Thinking about death makes his stomach churn with fear. To him, at this young age, death is something that would not come to him or any of his family but only to other people. Joining up to serve in the 'Army of Muhammad' seems to him a sure short route to death — even though the mujahidin sugar coat such deaths with the promise of heaven and the recipient of such death being treated as of a martyr for the holy cause — that is they never die but always live. But still, Siddiq could not find the courage to overcome his fear of being hit by a bullet from an Indian soldier and die without his loved ones being present around him. However, a part of Siddiq says that before succumbing to his fear of death and deciding on its bases, he should perform Salat al-Istikharah *(A prayer recited by Muslims to seek Allah's counsel for deciding on any issue in their life. The Prophet Muhammad asked Allah for guidance on matters important to him by praying very deep at night before going to bed. Allah then guided him in his sleep. Muhammad would either hear a whisper, a dream or would wake up with a pleasant or an ill feeling, helping him determine his next course of action).* In Siddiq's case, the guidance he seeks is whether to serve Allah by jihad or stay back with his family but still serve him.

Obviously, the fear factor involving death is the major reason behind him wanting to perform Salat al-Istikharah.

The dilemma Siddiq faces is such that if he performs Salat al-Istikharah and Allah commands him to join 'The Army of Muhammad', then there will be no going back. He knows very well that he will need to join the jihadis and risk having a bullet through his head from an Indian Soldier. So once he receives a 'yes' from Allah then he cannot simply ignore the Lord's command and not join 'The Army of Muhammad'. That will be treason. A huge disobedience to a direct order from his creator. The weight of such an occurrence will be too heavy for Siddiq to bear. He simply does not have the vile guts to carry out such disobedience. If he decides not to join without performing Salat al-Istikharah then he will be betraying himself and his morals. He has performed Salat al-Istikharah and sought Allah's guidance on matters important to him before: when he wasn't sure to take computer science or biology as his matriculation subject in school. So, not performing Salat al-Istikharah on this occasion would be a hypocritical act on his behalf. Siddiq thinks to himself that Allah abhors the hypocrites the most, even more than the non-believers, so I have no choice other than to perform Salat al-Istikharah.

Siddiq could feel the sweat around his knees and under his armpits. He is confused. He hears the Imam call 'Assalaam — au — alaikum Wa-rahmat-ullah', indicating the prayers have ended. He looks over his right shoulder and then his left, acknowledging both the unseen angels over his shoulders. He then looks at Adnan who gestures at him, asking him to come to the backyard of the mosque with him.

In a very confident tone, Adnan informs Siddiq about his decision. "I am performing the Salat al-Istikharah tonight, to ask Allah for his guidance on this matter. I hope he chooses me to serve him and makes me worthy of carrying out jihad for his name's sake." He then asks Siddiq by jerking his head forwards and opening his eyes as wide as he possibly could, "Siddiq, are you going to perform Salat al-Istikharah with me tonight?"

At first, Siddiq hesitates, but then replies hurriedly, "Yes! Yes of course..." although deep down he is not entirely sure...

4

"Another one of your sons sacrificed! O'Hussein[1]! How many more to follow? How many more?"

Both Kashif and his sister Zainab hold their mother, Madiha, by her shoulders while she cries these words out. The body of her husband and the kids' father, Dr. Zaidi, lies in front of them. Washed and wrapped like a toffee but in a white cloth instead of a wrapping foil. The corpse of Dr.Zaidi looks smaller than he physically was. Kashif has created an opening in the cloth around the face of the body. for the funeral. to see his father's face before he is buried into the ground. People come in turns to look at the dead man's face. Some are crying because of his untimely death and that he will be missed while others because this grim picture has taken their minds away from their mundane lives; the idea of death being a reality has suddenly hit them. But mostly, people looked at the deceased with controlled emotions and saying prayers for his soul to rest in peace and for it to reside in heaven till eternity.

A widow in her sixties says these words loudly for everyone in the funeral to hear but aims her words mainly for the deceased's wife, Madiha.

"Madiha, your husband is with Ahle-Bait *(Prophet Muhammad's Bloodline S.A)* now! Look at the calmness on his face. Ali-ibn-e-Abi Talib *(Phrophet's son-in-law and the rightful caliph according to Shiites)* has said, 'The only certain thing about life is death' and what can be a better death than to die as a martyr like Dr. Zaidi did! There is no guarantee that any of us can achieve this exaltation that Allah has gifted to your husband. Dr. Zaidi is truly blessed and it is a sin to call him dead. He lives amongst us as he is a martyr; don't we Shiites pray that one day the lord will bless us with the best possible death, which is martyrdom through the hands of our enemies? Your husband has just received that! His prayers have been answered, Madiha!"

These words are of little consolation for Madiha, who insisted her husband vacate the clinic as demanded by the Sipah-e-Sahaba. She knew very well that the group is made up of religious fanatics. She and Dr. Zaidi had long arguments about this situation. Dr. Zaidi kept underplaying the dangers posed by Sipah-e-Sahaba and delayed the move so that he can secure himself a clinic elsewhere first. On the contrary, Madiha kept pushing him to not worry too much about the financial loss incurred if he is to evacuate the clinic immediately, as no amount of money is worth his life. But Dr. Zaidi's calm assurances and his plan to move soon was enough to momentarily stop Madiha arguing with him. Now, with her husband lying dead in front of her, she blames herself for not pushing him hard enough on this matter. Guilt grips her along with fear of having to now move on with her life with two kids without the support of her husband.

"Kashif, this is probably not the right time but the Pakistan Central Intelligence Authority (CIA) are here."

Mehdi, Kashif's thirty-year-old cousin whispers these words to him while pulling him away slightly from Madiha.

"I mean Zulfiqar, our Shiite brother from CIA, is here. He wants to pass his condolences to you. Well, not just that; he says that he knows the asshole who did this to uncle Zaidi. Also, he knows the Sipah-e-Sahaba's ring leader for Orangi Town who ordered this attack in the first place. Zulfiqar wants to offer his help. He said he will have the motherfucker kidnapped and brought to you so that you can shoot him dead with your own hands, like he shot your father. Come with me to say hello to him."

Kashif does not want to give his complete attention to his cousin, Mehdi; in fact, his body language shows clear hesitation to meet Zulfiqar. He does not want to avenge his father death, although revenge was the first thought when he saw his father's dead body, but Kashif thought better of it. He wouldn't allow revenge or hate to consume his heart. He hasn't forgiven them or forgotten what these perpetrators have done to his father, causing so much grief to him and his family, but he has simply set himself free by not giving them any of these thoughts, may it be of hate. All Kashif wants now is to remember his father well and do right by his wish — that is to go to King's College London in United Kingdom, and study medicine.

Mehdi, sensing Kashif's reluctance to meet Zulfiqar, continues to speak to Kashif, but this time in a more rational tone. "I know you must be thinking what was taught to us by Maula Ali *(endearing reference to Ali-Ibn-e-Abi Talib by Shiites)* about revenge, that, 'The best deed of a great man is to forgive and forget'. But Kashif, we need to bring these men to justice. How many killers we all know that are out there and the Pakistani government has done nothing about it. Our CIA man, Zulfiqar, understands this and wants to help. Both myself and Zulfiqar want to do something for you, my brother. So please, come outside with me and just listen to what he has to say."

Kashif moves further away from his mother and turns towards his cousin, this time giving him not just his full attention but responds with a firm and a rather angry voice. "He who seeks vengeance must dig two graves: one for his enemy and one for himself. Have you ever heard of this Chinese proverb, my dear cousin? Shame, that even in this time of extreme difficulty, I need to rely on my own intellect to save myself from your stupid suggestions." Kashif says these words with authority, his chin facing down but his sorrowful eyes fixed at his cousin, Mehdi. With no further ado, he turns around to go back to his mother who is still not able to stop crying.

Moved by his cousin's words, Mehdi stops Kashif in his tracks by putting his hands warmly on his shoulder. "I'm sorry for your loss, Kashif, I really am and I'm also sorry to have brought this up at probably the wrong time. I know you are very upset and angry right now. I'll tell Zulfiqar that you passed your thanks to him and would see him some other time to discuss the options, maybe after the forty day mourning period? Ya Ali Madad! *(frequently used greeting among Shiites)*"

"No!" Visibly distressed, Kashif moves his cousin's hand away from his shoulder and gestures angrily asking Mehdi to withdraw with him to the adjacent room. In the next few seconds, Kashif tries his best to control his anger and not to be too hard on his cousin who is trying to help with good intention, but it is not what Kashif wants.

With not much success in overcoming his anger, he speaks to Mehdi in a commanding tone. "What options? I have told you that I am not interested. Zulfiqar can fuck off and so can you! Get this notion out of your head that you know what is best for me or any other Shiite out there. You only represent yourself and that too very badly! See what you have become: no family of your own, no real job and with friends like Zulfiqar who use you to be the face of their drug-selling business and offer you ridiculous advice! Please keep these advices to yourself, seriously! I mean it."

Stunned by Kashif's unexpected outburst, Mehdi doesn't know what to say so he keeps quiet.

Realizing that anger has taken the better of him, Kashif sighs and continues, "I know, cousin, that you are good at heart and I'm sorry if I am being rude to you but please try to understand that I don't see things the way you do. Right now, I just want to be left alone to find my own way. Do you know what my favourite quote from Maula Ali is? 'He who has the power to punish can only pardon.' So, even if you and Zulfiqar bring that man in front of me and give me a gun to shoot him dead, I will forgive him. And then all of your efforts will be in vain. So please tell Zulfiqar that I'm fine and if he wants to do something for me than he should pray for my dad and my family. And let that be the end of it."

Mehdi listens carefully and at the end gives Kashif a strong hug. "I am always here for you, little cousin, if you ever need me — you only need to pick up the phone. Ya Ali Madad!"

Kashif, who is now much calmer, replies in an amicable tone, "I know, thank you! Maula Ali Madad!"

As Kashif returns back to Madiha, he notices that she has now gone completely silent and appears to be in a state of trance. Kashif leans his head on her shoulder. Madiha's eyes are fixed on the calligraphic painting showing the holy names of the Panjtan Pak (that is the names of the Prophet Muhammad and his immediate family: Ali, Fatima, Hassan and Hussein). Although she appears to be in control, her eyes are turning red, showing intensity driven by grief and anger. The loss of her husband this early in her life was something that she has never prepared herself for. She does not know what to do and how to react now. She channels her emotion and, while staring at the picture, screams so loudly that Kashif almost jumps away from her,

"Why him? Why my husband? Why?"

This time, Kashif does not console Madiha, but instead he grips her shoulder by extending his arm around her back, and stood by her side. With a strong but a deep, low pitch voice, he whispers to her, "If there is someone or something to blame for my father's death, then it is 'religion', 'religion alone!' What has it achieved so far apart from slowing down the progress of mankind? I bet we were closer to God before the arrival of the so-called one and only true religion! Dad was a religious man but look what religion has given to him in return! He spent his days working hard to end the suffering of the sick, the poor and the vulnerable but what happened to him? Another religious man killed him, thinking that he will go to heaven for doing so! What is heaven anyway? A home for murderers and the oppressors?"

Madiha now turns her gaze away from the picture and looks at her son in the eyes. Kashif begins to feel apprehensive as he senses his mother's anger at the blasphemous words that he just uttered. Madiha does not agree with Kashif's outburst but she chooses not to react and does not utter a single word. It pains her more to see her son using this situation to turn himself away from religion, which herself and her deceased husband would never want. She briskly moves towards her husband's dead body and covers his face. As if she has regained all the self-control that she seemed to have lost, she gestures with her hand to the congregation that it is time for the burial proceedings to begin.

Dr. Zaidi was a very well-known man, this is evident by the number of people attending his funeral. The 'adhan', that is the call for the evening prayers, can be heard in the background now. This prompts the men that the funeral needs to start making their way towards the local Shiite mosque. Although the walk to the mosque is only five minutes, to march with the body on the shoulders may take longer. The evening prayers are due to begin fifteen minutes from the commencement of the adhan.

The men gather around the coffin and say loudly, "All praise be to Allah, his Prophet Muhammad and his family. All curse be to those who have wronged Allah, his Prophet and his Prophet's family."

They lift the coffin from the four corners on their shoulders and carry the body outside. Cries from both men and women are heard coming out from the house; Madiha weeps uncontrollably. The sound of crying is so frightening that the kids stop playing and rush back to their mothers. Kashif himself has goose bumps, but he calmly replaces the man holding the front right end of the coffin with his left shoulder. The funeral leaves the house and proceeds on foot to the Imam Bargah, the local Shiite mosque and reaches there on time in ten minutes.

The men rest the coffin on the front end of back courtyard and then they go inside with the Imam Bargah to pray, except for Kashif; he decides not to leave his father's corpse outside alone and stands next to the coffin. Kashif's childhood friend, Adeel, also stays behind to keep him company. Kashif sits on the ground, resting his back on the coffin, and Adeel sits down opposite.

Kashif then looks up to the sky and speaks slowly to Adeel. "I wonder, Adeel, whether it is better to be oppressed than to oppress? Because when you are being oppressed at least you have the sympathy of others. But what good is sympathy for anyway? Do you know what I mean?"

Adeel, a very polite and quiet natured boy nods his head in agreement and does not say anything. He has always been a good listener, a quality that Kashif admires in him the most.

Kashif continues to let his thoughts flow. "Look at the Americans now. People sympathized with them during 9/11, but when the Americans started their large-scale oppression in Afghanistan and Iraq, killing many civilians, the mood of the world towards the Americans changed. People began to dislike the Americans; no weapons of mass destruction were ever found in Iraq. Afghanistan turned into a killing field; Americans are now viewed as the aggressors or even oppressors. They destroyed these countries and turned them into barren lands which now breeds more extremists than before!"

Kashif sighs and looks at Adeel, who is still listening intently, so he continues, "When the Romans conquered any town or a city, whether big or small, they developed it, they made its people feel useful. So did the Greeks, the French and the British. Look at our country. Pakistan's railway system, schools, hospitals or any other strong functional buildings — I bet you they were all made by the British when they were here. But, unfortunately, the Americans did not do that in Afghanistan and Iraq as needed. They did not stay there long enough to know the people and work with them to develop their country. I think America now faces similar dislike from people that the Germans faced after the holocaust of Jews. If there is such a thing as karma then it will get those American leaders and they will need to pay for the oppression they carried out on innocent civilians.

"I'm saying all this because I believe the same will happen to the killer of my father. I don't need to avenge him — karma will get him. If I waste an iota of my life thinking about avenging my father's death, then that will destroy my soul. My father wanted me to study medicine at King's College London. He even helped me to fill out the application form, paid the tuition fee, boarding, lodging, everything. He wouldn't want me to waste my time here with these imbeciles and seek revenge. I will go to London, my dear friend — I will fulfil my father's dream and make him proud! I will leave all the anger behind me and start fresh. There is a world out there and I want to live it! And I know that only this positivity will bring peace to my father's soul."

5

It is coming up to midnight but the gates of the Abu Bakar mosque are still open for the worshippers. The streets of Karachi are buzzing with life. People have stayed up late either to pray or to shop for the nearing festivity of Eid. Around this time of the year, the shop keepers work on a different time scale. They sleep during the day while they fast and work from Iftar, which is late evening, till Sehri i.e. the early hours of the next morning. So, one can say they work from dusk to almost dawn. The atmosphere inside the mosque is also lively with the worshipper busy performing the namaaz or reading the Quran, asking Allah for more blessings.

The last ten days of Ramadan sees many worshippers visiting and, in some cases, camping inside the mosque overnight to perform additional prayers. They believe that the blessings from Allah are multiplied in large numbers during these ten days as according to the Quran and the Prophet, Ramadan is Allah's favourite month and that the Prophet Muhammad himself visited the heavens and the hell in one of these last ten nights of this holy month called 'The Shab-e-Qadar'. The exact night is not known for certain, but it is widely believed to be the odd nights, that is from the twenty-first to twenty-ninth of the month. Prophet's visit to these places are described in the Quran and by the Islamic scholars, bearing similarities between Dante's famous *Inferno* and

Paradiso. The Prophet Muhammad also then met Allah and conversed with him. According to some Shiite scholars, Allah used Ali Ibn-e-Abi Talib's voice to communicate with the Prophet, which is disputed by their opposite Sunni numbers. That would give Ali Ibn-e-Abi Talib a status of a deity himself or, if not, then someone who is closer to Allah than the Prophet; so one begins to understand why this is considered contentious.

As the actual night 'The Shab-e-Qadar' is still not known, some Muslims pray during all the last ten nights to ensure that they haven't missed out on claiming their share of bounty by not praying during the holiest night of the Islamic calendar. To accommodate the increased number of worshippers staying overnight, mosque committees lay out the camps inside the premises. The camps are very basic — effectively, four plain white curtains hanging from the ropes spread across the width and length of the hall beneath the ceiling, with room enough for one single sleeping bed. This year, seven members of the Jaish-e-Mohammad ('The Army of Muhammad'), led by Uthman, along with other twenty-two local worshippers, including Siddiq and Adnan, have vowed to camp in the mosque for the last ten days of Ramadan.

Siddiq has difficulty sleeping. The lights inside the mosque do not go off during the night, for most of the worshippers stay awake all night reading the Quran and praying. Although Siddiq has been sleeping well with the same amount of light for the past six nights, tonight, having finished the prayers around ten p.m., he has since been tossing and turning on the floor in his camp bed. Clearly, it is not that brightness of the surroundings; his decision not to perform

Salat al-Istikharah, in order to seek Allah's guidance on the matter of joining 'The Army of Muhammad', is keeping him awake. Also, his plan to lie to his friend, Adnan, in the morning that he did perform Salat al-Istikharah but hasn't received any answer from Allah, is further playing on his conscience and keeping him awake. He thinks to himself, 'It is the fear of dying more so than anything else that is making me not ask Allah on this matter and lie to my friend'. He rationalizes his feelings by saying to himself, "It is better to be a coward than to be a hypocrite — that is, not join 'The Army of Muhammad', even though Allah asks me to. And if Allah does command me to join 'The Army of Muhammad' then I will not question it and just join no matter how scared I am! So all I am doing now is avoiding asking Allah this question, in case I get a reply that I am not ready to act upon."

With his camp bed on the floor surrounded by loosely hanging curtains, Siddiq is able to peep outside easily by lifting the bottom part of the curtains. Among others, he sees Adnan sat in the front row, moving back and forth while reciting the Quran. There is a small group of people sat in a circle at the far-right corner, talking to Uthman. Being fed-up of his conscience irritating him and keeping him awake, Siddiq decides finally to perform the Salat al-Istikharah and take the risk of having to join 'The Army of Muhammad'. He kicks off the quilt, stands up and moves next to his bed to pray...

The night has passed. It is still dark and uncharacteristically cold for an October morning. Siddiq has managed to sleep peacefully through the night. He is woken up by the sound of an alarm that echoes inside the hall of the mosque to indicate that it is time for Sehri, a meal consumed early in the morning before fasting. He drags himself out of the bed. Feeling cold, he puts on his jumper and walks gingerly towards the toilets. As he is just about to take the steps down the open-air veranda, he sees Adnan coming out of the toilet. Adnan looks at Siddiq and immediately his face brightens up; he rushes to meet Siddiq half way on the stairs. "Allah has spoken to me, Siddiq! I had a dream last night…" Adnan tries his best to control any more words coming out from his mouth.

Siddiq tries to show Adnan his utmost interest even at this early hour and with the cold. He wraps his arms across on top of each other and squeezes his palms between his armpits. With a distinctive shiver in his voice, he tries hopelessly to match Adnan's enthusiasm. "Tell me, Adnan, what was your dream like?"

Seeing that Siddiq is shivering due to cold weather, Adnan holds Siddiq by his shoulders, and with his trademark wide smile, continues, "I want to tell this to Uthman first but don't worry, my friend! I will tell you later. All I can tell you now, is that the dream was a clear sign from Allah asking me to join 'The Army of Muhammad' and I woke up with a very pleasant and happy feeling this morning! Now you are very cold, Siddiq — I will catch up you after the prayers."

Siddiq acknowledges and continues walking down the stairs. Adnan suddenly shouts back at him, "Hey, what about you? Did you have any dreams?"

Siddiq doesn't turn around but shakes his head sideways, gesturing that he has not heard anything from Allah during the night.

Adnan hurries towards Uthman's camp. He cannot wait to tell him about his dream with each and every detail. The fact that he believes that Allah has spoken to him in his dream is an overwhelming ordeal for him. Even though some scepticism creeps in his mind that Allah is unconceivable by the human mind and the chances of him speaking to Adnan in Urdu language is slim, he shrugs off the scepticism by saying to himself, "Allah can do whatever he wants, plus there are other elements in my dream that can be interpreted as a clear sign."

So, with some conviction, Adnan marches towards Uthman's camp. Just outside the camp he sees a queue of about five people already waiting to see Uthman. He says to a man just ahead of him, who appears to be in his late twenties, "Five o'clock in the morning. I thought I would have no problem seeing him. But there are four of you already ahead of me!"

The man nods his head in agreement and replies, "I came about ten minutes before you and the queue hasn't moved an inch. People who come to tell Uthman their dreams or how they slept after performing Salat al-Istikharah, must have had good reasons to come here, otherwise why would anyone come here to whine to Uthman that Allah doesn't want them to be a part of his holy army?"

Adnan sighs and blinks his eyes, slowly suggesting that he agrees with the man. Before he could ask the man what kind of dream he had, the curtain of Uthman's camp slides open. A rather contented-looking man comes out smiling ahead of Uthman, followed by Uthman himself.

Uthman looks at the queue of people for him and says in a crisp friendly voice, "My beloved brothers, believe me, I am as eager to listen to your true dreams as you are eager to tell them to me. Patience is our greatest virtue. I'm afraid it is almost time for Fajr *(morning)* prayers and I haven't had a chance to eat before the time for Sehri ends. We will need to postpone this session for after the prayers, my beloved Muslims. Peace be upon you."

He moves back inside his camp without making any further eye contact with anyone. People scatter and so does Adnan. Watching Uthman from a close distance has driven away his anxiousness to blurt out his dream to him. Instead, he now contemplates receiving direct orders from the man that he finds himself in awe of. 'I will do anything that he asks of me,' Adnan whispers to himself.

There is an unusual buzz in the Abu Bakr mosque this morning. As many worshippers have performed Salat al-Istikharah and interpreting their dreams, either by themselves or sharing them with others or with Uthman. Siddiq eats his Sehri meal with an acquaintance of his called Nabil, a mechanical engineering student who is camped next to him. Nabil is among the growing number of youngsters in Karachi who try to balance time between acquiring professional qualifications alongside religious practices. The latter involving praying five times a day, devoting at least an hour of the day to reading and understanding the Quran and at least an hour a day preaching to other fellow Muslims in the area as to how to become better Muslims. Nabil is on the chubby side, and being not very tall, some of his mates refer to him as short and fat. He has a very dark brown complexion with a reasonably long black beard and short hair, covered most of the time by the Islamic white cap worn in most parts of the sub-continent. He also wears his trousers above the ankle like many other Muslims because some scholars have been quoting Prophet Muhammad, saying, 'Wearing whatever is below the ankles may drive one to hell'.

"I heard a voice during my sleep last night, Siddiq", says the twenty-one-year-old Nabil. In his customary way, Nabil brings over his food to Siddiq's camp every morning as they share each other's meals sent over to them by their families. He continues, "It said, I should do jihad and I will be forgiven. It kept echoing in my head. I don't know how many times it repeated."

Siddiq is unable to find the right words to say or even to carry an easy-going face expression. His eyes show a mixture of forced happiness but predominantly concern.

So, he asks, "What are you going to do about it then?".

Nabil replies in an authoritative tone, "Nothing, Siddiq."

"What do you mean nothing, Nabil? The message is clear. Allah is asking you to do jihad! So you should." Siddiq let his feelings known to Nabil.

"That is correct, Siddiq. Allah this ask me to do jihad but that could mean any form of jihad. Even helping one's parents in their old age is jihad, according to Prophet Muhammad. Not always one needs to pick up a sword or a gun and go fight the enemy. I mean, that is not the only form of jihad! So it is indeed very clear to me that from now on, my every action, my every breath will be for Allah, and therefore my whole life will be a jihad."

Siddiq disagrees with the interpretation that Nabil has just made by himself, but tries not to object. To Siddiq, it is clear that Nabil has received a direct order from Allah asking him to join The Army of Muhammad and he is rationalizing a way out here for himself. Siddiq continues to think that Nabil is simply twisting the meaning of the message of the voice to his own liking and being a smart ass. He seems to have forgotten that he asked Allah for guidance on the matter of joining Uthman and 'The Army of Muhammad', not whether he should help out his parents when they are old! He has another brother to take care of that, surely! If I had received such a voice in my sleep, I would have been knocking at Uthman's door like Adnan must be doing right now. Nabil is nothing but a spineless hypocrite!

Being annoyed, Siddiq finally asks Nabil, "Aren't you going to tell this dream of yours to Uthman, at least, and see what he makes of it?".

"No, I'm not going to tell him, Siddiq, I don't see the need. I know what Allah wants from me." Nabil tears the foil from the top of the big bowl filled with lamb biryani. "Here you go, Siddiq — have some to celebrate the voice! And by the way, sorry, I totally forgot to ask you. Did you have any dreams?".

Siddiq pulls out a spoon from the side of the bag containing his food, digs into the biryani and casually replies, "Allah doesn't speak to me, Nabil, like he does to you! And if he did than I'll do exactly what he says without making my own little interpretation of it that suits me." He continues to stuff his mouth with food to avoid any further conversation with Nabil.

"Tell me, my young angel — how did you sleep last night?" Uthman puts his palm reassuringly on Adnan's shoulder.

Adnan's face lights up with confidence following Uthman's fatherly demeanour. He replies, "Allah spoke to me last night! I saw that I was surrounded by men who wore black scarfs on their heads, dark sunglasses on their eyes, bodies draped in khakis and held brown coloured rifles. First, they asked me what I am doing here. 'I want to cross this hill so I can go to my home', I said.

One of the men, who I distinctly remember was very short and fat, shouted at me, saying that I am a Muslim and I should leave this land immediately and go back to where I belong, otherwise, he'll kill me! The other men started to push me away from the back of their rifles at the same time. Then the fat man laughed loudly and says to me in a mean voice, while spitting on my face, 'You fool, what home do you speak of? Don't you know we have burned your house down with your family inside it! We raped all your women, one by one, and then killed them'!

At that time, I snatched the rifles from one of the men and started shooting blindly. They fired back at me but, miraculously, all the bullets missed me. I killed them all, one by one, even the fat one. In fact, I shot him three times in his stomach after I shot him in his head first. His belly flapped like a huge wave each time I shot him in the stomach. Then suddenly, from the top of the hill, I heard two other men shouting something that I didn't understand. I saw that they were armed with machine guns. I dropped my rifle and ran for my life. They started shooting and again, miraculously, none of the bullets hit me. But this time, I felt really scared as I knew it is only a matter of time when one of the bullets will hit me in the back or in the back of my skull. Running with cold hands and feet, I came near the edge of the cliff and suddenly there were no bullets being fired. I stopped and looked back for a second. They were loading their guns. I looked down and about fifty feet below there was a fresh water river flowing at a rate of knots. Knowing that this is my only chance of survival, I jumped. And there were gun shots again. The bullets pierced through my shawl as it lifted up in the air while gravity pulled my body towards the river. At this point, I woke up knowing I had survived."

Uthman kisses Adnan on his forehead and says, "I welcome you to 'The Army of Muhammad', my little angel! May the blessings of Allah be with you from now on, brother Adnan." At this point, Uthman pulls out the Holy Quran covered in red velvet cloth with golden strings and brings it in front of Adnan. "I must ask you now, Adnan, to take the oath. However, remember that you have a choice now to either go back to the world, disobeying your Allah, or put your hand on the Quran in front of these two Mujahideen present and swear by the Allah that you will serve 'The Army of Muhammad' with your life and with unwavering bravery. And I, Uthman bin Aziz, am your supreme commander who you will obey under all circumstances without question. Or else, like I said before, you could just walk out now instead, with a burdened soul, and never see us again. We won't come after you or hold any umbridge but you will have to live with yourself Adnan, if you know what I mean…"

Adnan, without wasting a second and with no second thoughts, puts his hand on the Holy Quran and repeats, "I swear by Allah that I will obey Uthman bin Aziz, my supreme commander, with bravery, loyalty and complete obedience. I will not fear death and will hope to die as a martyr fighting the enemies of Allah and his Prophet Muhammad."

"Masha-Allah! Welcome to 'The Army of Muhammad', our brother mujahid, Adnan Marhaba!" Uthman cries out loudly, with a smile, and then hugs Adnan.

6

"I am extremely sorry for your loss, Kashif. Please, let me know if I can do anything for you guys — I really mean it!"

Omar says that with utmost sincerity in his voice and hugs Kashif. He has arrived late in the afternoon, when most of the people present at the burial service have already left. Kashif, who now feels very tired, nods his head in agreement but does not reply. Kashif's dark black hair is usually gelled together and pulled behind to give a nice slick look. At five feet ten inches tall, athletic body, pointy nose, strong jaw bone and hazel eyes, Kashif does not lack admirers of the opposite sex. These days, however, he has left his hair without any styling products so it takes a shape of bush made from his curls. Also, having not shaved for a few days, his dark black facial hair is somewhat in between a stubble and a beard, making him look older than he actually is. Still, he seems to be able to draw attention from other females whenever he happens to be around them.

"How is your mother, Kashif? Where is she?"

Kashif realizes that they are having this one-sided conversation at the entrance door, so he replies with an apology. "Sorry, Uncle Omar, please come in. Mother is in the drawing room with other family women. You can meet her there…"

Omar looks away from Kashif and towards his house and begins to work out in his head whether it would be appropriate to go amongst the women as some might do hijab and wouldn't appreciate the presence of a man other than their husbands or immediate family.

Kashif, pre-empting Omar's thoughts, cleverly and swiftly puts Omar's mind at ease. "It is fine — everyone is meeting her there. She hasn't moved from there since the funeral left the house. But please be careful when you speak to her, Omar uncle. She is not being herself today and might burst into uncontrollable episodes of crying."

Omar acknowledges and readies himself to see Dr. Zaidi's wife, Madiha. The woman that he has always fancied. "I understand that, Kashif, please do not worry. I don't expect her to be herself today or in the next coming few days — it is only normal. That is why — if you need any help, even in terms of dealing with your mother, then let me know. I'll ask Layla to come along with me next time. She wanted to come with me today but I kept her at home as she just returned from the hospital today with our new-born, Ali. She sends her condolences — I'll pass them on to your mother."

Kashif leads Omar into the drawing room where a handful of women are sat reciting the Quran for the deceased. Madiha is sat amongst them; she has a prayer bead in her hands instead of the Quran. She has a fair complexion and her beautiful skin looks fresh, even without any makeup. Her eyelids have turned pink because of crying. She is dressed in black and has covered her hair with a black shawl. Omar finds her strangely angelic, mostly covered in black shalwar kameez and dupatta[1] around her head. Her face, with hazel eyes, feet and hands are the only parts of the body that Omar can see. She has kept her gaze fixed on the ground. Omar notices that she is holding the first bead in her hand and hasn't dropped it while her lips constantly move as if she is talking intensely to some imaginary person lying on the floor. Kashif holds Omar's hand and tries to take him closer to her so that she might notice them. Instead, Omar pulls Kashif's hand back. "Wait!" Omar feels that it is inappropriate to breach Madiha's concentration. More so, he is intimidated by the strong aura he senses around Dr. Zaidi's wife. At the same time, he finds her extremely attractive to an extent that he begins to feel tingling in his testicles. "Let it be, Kashif — I don't think it is a good time to disturb her. I'll come again soon and will bring Layla with me."

Omar leaves the house and gets into his car — a shiny new Honda Civic with black leather seats and black exterior. He turns on the air conditioning to maximum and opens his golden cigarette case, which is almost empty. He then takes out a shiny silver zippo from his kurta pocket, expertly lights it in the first attempt, inhales his Dunhill cigarette and then shuts the lid of zippo with a swift jerk of the wrist. He puts his automatic car into drive and starts off slowly. He keeps thinking about Dr. Zaidi's wife. 'She looked so goddamn attractive! I'd like to shag her once at least or maybe have an affair with her. I can't be with her permanently, of course! But holding her body in my arms would be so incredible'! He sighs with a little smoke still coming out from his mouth and nostrils. He inhales deeply, enjoying the cool air from the air conditioning mixed with the smell of leather and cigarette. Omar, although tall, muscular and dark in complexion, never seemed to catch the attention of Dr. Zaidi's wife in a way that he would've wanted. He believes that it is probably the moustache that puts her off him completely. 'I still don't think that I can get rid of my moustache just for her but if that gets me in bed with her than why not give it a try'? He kills the cigarette in the ash tray and turns up the volume of the audio CD playing, *Afreen, Afreen* by Nusrat Fateh Ali Khan.

These are very special days at Omar's house. His parents cannot get enough of the newborn, Ali. Layla is not allowed, by his parents, to exert herself in any house chores until she recovers fully from her post-delivery tiredness, although Layla has explained a number of times to her in-laws that she does not feel tired at all now. Layla, in fact, endearingly complains to her mother-in-law that with all this delicious and rich food around her she can only become fat and Omar would leave her for another woman.

Layla has decided to join the nearby gym that has women-only dedicated hours in the afternoon every day. Looking good and staying fit has been very important to Layla since her first boyfriend left her for a prettier girl. She was only about eighteen years old at the time. To date, she recalls how she joined the same engineering university as her ex-boyfriend so that she could be closer to him and possibly win him back. Instead, she found him running around pretty girls like a hungry dog drooling from his mouth when it sees food. That was when she decided to work on her looks and to get attention from anyone that she fancied or not.

With her sharp features and attractive plump breasts, it didn't take her long to start gaining attention from the hunks and popular guys around her, especially when she wore skin-tight clothes. She felt that her hard work in the gym had finally paid off when, at the university's annual dinner party, her ex-boyfriend came up to her and confessed, "Shallow as it may sound, Layla, but I find it unfortunate that you realised how important good looks in a girl are to me only when I've left you. Look at you now! You have never looked this sexy before! Would you blame me now that I regret leaving you and want you back again?! I can't help but think that by looking this hot you only wanted to prove to me that I am shallow and make me regret my decision to leave you. Just so you know, Layla, I lament on my stupidity to leave you back then but believe me, Layla, I want you now, more than ever before! I fancy you very much." That night they had sex in one of the empty unlocked classrooms inside the university's electrical department. After that, Layla told him that she has moved on and does not want to see him again.

Omar honks the car just outside the main gate of his house and within seconds the gates are opened by the servant and Omar drives in. His house is a two-story bungalow with a detached entrance to the first floor where he and Layla live with their two children. Omar's mother and father both live on the ground floor. His father receives a state pension. He retired as a grade twenty custom officer. His father also owns one of the luxury apartments overlooking the sea which is rented out to a young couple and he receives a handsome monthly rent from them. The family is well-to-do and Omar is well known in the Defence Housing Authority area as a Nimco manufacturer and supplier — a snack made up of mainly dried lentils, peanuts, chickpeas, flour noodles and spices. Omar goes inside the house but chooses to stay with his parents. He decides to have a conversation with them to divert his mind away from thinking about Dr. Zaidi's wife before going upstairs to see his own.

"I remember very clearly, as a child, when we used to live in Gulberg Town, that the Imam of the Abu Bakr mosque told us that Christians, Jews or people belonging to other religions or no religion at all, cannot be our true friends. For these people will always have their own agenda which is very different to ours."

Omar starts talking to his mother while she chops vegetables in the kitchen. She is almost seventy, with no debilitating illness, unlike her husband, who has already survived a severe heart attack. She feels herself close to God and since her menopause, has prayed five times a day without missing a single prayer.

Omar, knowing that he has her listening ear, continues, "After Dr. Zaidi's death, I don't know what to believe any more. His killer was his own patient, believing in the same Allah and the same Prophet, but still brutally murdered him!"

Omar's mother replies in a casual but assertive tone, trying to show to him that it all makes sense to her,

"Dr. Zaidi was a Shia and you know very well that Shiites believe that Ali should have been the last Prophet instead of Muhammad. They idolize Ali; some even say that Allah spoke to Muhammad in Ali's voice and the hand that shook Muhammad's hand when he was above the seven skies meeting Allah, was that of Ali! This is blasphemy. And Shiites get punished by Allah for having such ridiculous beliefs!"

Omar is visibly angry by his mother comments and replies hastily in a challenging tone, "So you think that the green turban sister fucker was right in killing Dr. Zaidi?" and before his mother could reply, he continues, "You speak about the topics that you don't know anything about with such confidence — that can only mean that you are a fool! Shiites don't believe all of that and also, they never killed anyone. It was disturbing what you've just said — I don't know why I spoke to you about my feelings anyway — I hate being weak."

He turns around and leaves the kitchen immediately to go upstairs to his wife. His mother, unfazed and unimpressed by her son's burst of anger, continues to put the chopped vegetables in the cauldron of boiling water as she prepares vegetable soup for her husband.

On the way up the stairs, Omar encounters Layla coming downstairs wearing tights, trainers and a brown shawl that covers her body from the neck down to just over her knees. "I didn't think you will be back this early. You don't look very well. Are you ok? How was the funeral?" Layla asks Omar.

"It was okay, my love — where are you off to?" Omar quickly changes the topic.

"Please don't be mad at me but I'm going to the gym to renew my membership. I have become so fat. I need to do something about it. And don't worry, I won't push too hard! I have done a lot of that recently — pushing our baby boy out from my little hole..." Layla smiles and rightly pre-empts Omar's concern about recovering from her pregnancy.

Omar sharply replies, "You look gorgeous, sweetheart, and not fat at all, but if it will make you feel good then go for it. And I will tell you about the funeral when you come back. Madiha and the kids are understandably very upset but time will heal everything, like it always does. Anyway, go and enjoy but don't put yourself under too much stress."

Omar feels relieved that he would have more time to himself to gather his thoughts regarding Madiha. He assumes that the kids are being looked after by their maid and Layla, as if reading Omar's mind, confirms. "Ali is asleep, the little princess is playing on the computer and the maid is cleaning the bookshelf. Food is cooked; just microwave it if you are hungry."

Layla kisses Omar goodbye and then sits in the back seat of the family car and is then chauffeured off to the gym.

7

"Stand still, breathe deep and remain silent! You will slowly begin to see through this dense fog. Then keep looking until you see a number of street lamps concentrated in a small area. Make a good note of that, register that not only in your heads but also in your hearts. It is the Indian army headquarters. This is where all the scumbags live. Soon, a chosen few of you will be paying them a visit that they will never live to remember!"

Uthman delivers these words of advice to the four new recruits, including Adnan, who are trying their best to follow his instructions in order to get a sight of the Indian army headquarters. The fog is settling down on the grounds of Badgam near Srinagar *(City within the Indian territory of Jammu and Kashmir)*. It is only five p.m. but the sun has disappeared, leaving it pitch dark. Although tired from the non-stop journey in the back of a Toyota Hilux from Islamabad to Rawalakot, followed by hours of crawling through the tunnel, the boys are still keen to impress Uthman, who they have fully accepted as their supreme commander and spiritual leader.

Uthman, looking in the direction of the headquarters, continues to speak to the boys. "Time, give it some time, my soldiers — you will begin to see. Your heart is beating too fast and your muscles are very tense. Relax! You are not here to be judged or marked like you were used to in your schools. Now, you are the soldiers of Allah and only He the Almighty will judge you. And believe me, Allah recognizes the sacrifices you have already made to come here and join this holy war. The war in which there are no worldly medals to be won, no promotions or pay rises to be had and neither will there be a Remembrance Day for you when you die. In fact, you may not even receive a proper Muslim burial and your dead bodies might never be found! The only reward you will receive will be from Allah. And what reward can be better than the reward from Allah? For the Almighty will open the gates of heaven for you! There, you will drink the purest water, honey & alcohol from the hands of Prophet Muhammad himself. There will be endless bounty including seventy-two beautiful virgins for your enjoyment, and with them you can have coitus for as long as you want. This is all guaranteed to you by Allah in his heaven, regardless of whether you survive this and live as heroes in your Lord's eyes or die fighting for him as martyrs."

He then turns around to face the recruits and continues in a warm fatherly tone, "The path we are treading now is narrow and long. We will go on this journey together but then each of us will meet our own individual destiny. My advice to you is to keep your faith only in Allah and you will stay above the water. If, at any point, you fear death or your enemy or anything else other than Allah then you will surely drown.

"So, stand erect and be fearless. When you find yourself in battle with the enemy, do what the great warriors of Islam like Omar-bin-Khattab *(the second Caliph of Muslims)* and Ali Ibn-e-Abi-Talib did; grit your teeth and keep your eyes fixed at the farthest enemy line as your target to reach. Then move forward with purpose and kill every enemy that comes in between you and your target. Remember to be kind to women and children, the old and the sickly, when you encounter them. The women here are beautiful like the place itself but remember one thing — 'Women are like scorpions whose grip is sweet'[4]. They have lured some of our men into honey traps and got them captured by the Indian army. In return, they got themselves a handsome reward. So, be on your guard against them and never make that mistake. We will not come to your help in such a case. If you do find a woman that you fancy, marry her and bring her to the camp, but under no circumstances she will be allowed to leave the camp then. Enough said. Let's go back to the camp now and have some rest. Tomorrow you will be briefed on your first mission.

It has already been a week since the new recruits have arrived near the 'line of control' in the Pakistan-administered Azad Kashmir. They live in a three-storey house in a village at the outskirts of Muzaffarabad. The house has no telecommunication or internet facility of any kind. In fact, it does not even have electricity. They have to burn candles for light and use a gas cylinder for cooking and boiling water. The battery-powered fans are there to provide cool air during the afternoon. The recruits are constantly monitored, for any suspicious activities, by spies working for 'The Army of Muhammad'. In this case, the spies look out for any signs of non-extremism or irresolution towards the jihadi cause; or something as simple as showing liking towards the Western culture, trying to escape or speak to strangers in the area, or any other signs of weakness in their resolve to serve in 'The Army of Muhammad'.

On the first day when they arrived, they were given their own Russian-made pistols and a crash course on how to use them by a skilled Taliban fighter. On subsequent days, after the morning prayers, the recruits were escorted to a deserted playground between the hills where they were subjected to gruelling military-style fitness training. The training lasted till just before afternoon prayers. The final task was to shoot a round of AK47 at a target, which, surprisingly, none of the new recruits excelled at. They were then treated to a lentil curry, boiled eggs, chopped fresh vegetables and naan bread. The desert was a simple dish made of rice pudding and black tea was served in the end. The recruits were allowed an hour nap after the noon prayers and were then woken up to engage themselves in Quran recital till the evening prayers. After the recital, the recruits would meet other members of 'The Army of Muhammad' in the local school auditorium that had been converted into a makeshift mosque in the evening. The Imam from 'The Army of Muhammad' then delivers his sermon where he tells stories of the lives of the Prophet Muhammad and his followers. The stories were carefully selected — they would talk about the struggles faced by the Prophet against the non-believers and they would normally end with a promise of reward from Allah. Can we put a story here?

The Imam would bring the sermon to close by focusing on the importance of jihad and promoting hatred for the West and bringing to light the atrocities carried out by the Indian army on the Muslims of Kashmir. After the sermon, the new recruits, along with the other frontline fighters, were served with dinner while Uthman, along with the senior members and the Imam, would depart to the adjacent room and discuss their strategy and plan of attack.

Adnan walks in a straight line, with the other recruits, behind Uthman. He is slightly confused as to why Uthman spoke so much about women and marriage. He leans over to the recruit in front of him while they approach the tunnel and whispers in his ear, "I am here only to fight and die as a martyr. I have never had intercourse so naturally I don't miss it! I don't want to come out of here alive as a hero; I need a mission that guarantees me death as a martyr so that I can meet Allah, the most beneficial and merciful. I would rather lose my virginity up there with the true virgins than with any woman here!" The recruit, who seems out of breath, keeps his head down and continues to walk without a reply.

They stop at the tunnel dug by the Mujahideens. Unknown to the Indian authorities, the tunnel goes under the line of control and links the Poonch district on the Indian-administered side of Kashmir to Rawalakot on the Pakistan-administered side of Kashmir. Uthman shouts loudly enough for the group to hear, "As I told you before, once we are in the tunnel we cannot stop. The only way is forward! You have five minutes to get yourselves ready. Make sure you urinate now. As before, in the tunnel, keep your torches in your mouth and then tune your hearts to say 'Allah ho Akbar' — the time will pass easily."

Exactly five minutes later, Uthman leads the recruits into the tunnel. They start crawling behind him, knowing that they need to put their heads down, for at least a good, few hours now. Adnan and the rest of the boys follow Uthman's advice to the letter. Some of the boys have tuned their hearts so well that while they inhale, a muffled sound of 'Allah' is heard, then 'ho Akbar' when they exhale, creating rhythmic chant of 'Allah ho Akbar' meaning 'God is great'. Adnan feels the adrenaline pumping through his veins. He is ready to fight — a feeling so strong that he wants to turn around and ambush the Indian army headquarters right away.

He recalls how his older brother, who was notorious to have street fights during cricket matches with teams of other neighbourhoods, said that, 'It gives me more pleasure to win a street fight then the cricket match itself! I cannot describe the feeling to you, my little brother — you have to experience it'. Adnan slowly begins to associate with the feeling that his brother mentioned.

He then recalls what his brother had told him the night before he left with Uthman. 'Adnan, I was at the barber today. He wrapped a black cloth around my neck and then began clipping my hair. I was tired so kept my eyes down on the cloth.'

Adnan remembers interfering candidly by saying, 'For obvious reasons, and that is you cannot afford to look straight into the mirror to witness your ugly face'!

But his brother continued with grave seriousness. 'There were distinctive amounts of white hair that fell on the cloth along with the black ones. Black hair, Adnan, it was always black hair falling on the cloth the last time I recall keeping my eyes down on the cloth and looking at them. Life has passed me by in one big hurry. I even remember the time when you were little and I used to take you with me to school. I thought I'm still young, you are still my baby brother, Mom and Dad will always be fit and healthy and everything will stay as it is.

But just seeing my own white hair falling on the cloth has shown me just how fast life changes in front of our eyes! And most of the times we are blind and unable to see. My little brother, go and do what you must do, what pleases you and what makes you have no regrets. Because one day, this will happen to you too; you will see white hair falling down from your head — I want you to have done what you always wanted to do by then'.

Feeling the warmth of the hug that he gave to his brother before saying goodbye, Adnan finds his torch falling from his mouth as it hits the feet of the boy in front of him as they all come to a stop. They have crossed the tunnel and Uthman has started to climb up the ropey ladder. Adnan whispers to himself, "You were right, brother. Time flies faster than we realize!"

8

"You boarding pass please, sir!"

The petite airhostess with big dark black eyes and long curved eyelashes directs Kashif towards his aisle seat. The Emirates Boeing 777 bound to Dubai from Karachi is filled mostly by people taking connecting flights to Europe or America. Kashif's destination is London. He is due to start his course studying medicine at King's College London in two weeks' time. Although his father, Dr. Zaidi, has already paid for the tuition fee and kept money aside for his boarding and lodging, Kashif has decided to leave all the money behind for his mother and sister. The money is not necessarily needed by Madiha as she has already received a handsome amount from the life insurance of her deceased husband. Still, Kashif believed in leaving an extra sum of money behind for his family rather than to take it with him to England. He has only taken enough to cover his flight to the UK and a meagre sum of a thousand pounds cash to give him a start in the UK until he finds some work. Although Kashif has unwavering intentions to fulfil his own and his father's wishes to study at King's College, he is willing to work hard to support himself financially as well. He sees this as an opportunity to become independent and eventually support his family.

Kashif has spoken to his former schoolmate, Faisal, who is already living in London for the past two years as a student, to help him with accommodation when he arrives. Faisal is very kind in demeanour and has offered to pick Kashif up from the airport. He is registered as a full-time student at Stratford International College in East London but works at two jobs in order to send money back to his family in Pakistan. He has welcomed Kashif wholeheartedly. The two-bedroom house where Faisal lives, in Glen Park Road in Forest Gate, East London, already has five men from Karachi living in it, including Faisal. Kashif's addition would add nicely as both the rooms will have three men each; two sleeping on the bed and one on the floor. It will also mean that the rent and bills will have a bigger dividing factor and that will increase the monthly savings of the other five men.

Faisal and his housemates are from a reasonably well-off neighbourhood in Karachi; they all have reasonable academic qualifications which would easily get them a white collar job in Pakistan but they chose to venture out to the UK in pursuit of quick money as, with the high exchange rate, the money earned in the UK sums up to over a hundred times in Pakistan. All the men in the house, apart from Kashif, took the same path to arrive in the UK. They applied to study for an MBA Programme at the same Stratford International College in East London. The subject that they chose for the MBA was unique and one that is not offered in any university in Pakistan. The men used this fact to convince the UK visa officers in Pakistan to obtain a student's visa to travel to the UK. The intention of these men, were never to actually study for a degree in the UK but to come here to have some fun, work, make a bit of money and send it back home in Pakistan. The owner of the Stratford International College is a middle-aged man from Bangladeshi origin, born in UK. He takes two thousand pounds from each of these men annually in order to give them fake passing grades, attendance sheets and other relevant paperwork required to prove to the visa authorities that they have been attending college regularly, when actually these men spend most of their time working at superstores, namely Tesco and Sainsburys. These fake documents, on original letterheads and certificates, help the men for their visa extensions whenever due. Not only this, but with an extra thousand pounds at the end of the course, the college will issue these men their fake MBA degrees with a pass grade, obviously without submitting course work or sitting in exams. All of the men living in the house work six days a week on minimum wage or slightly higher, but because they share all the bills, they manage to save good money and are even able to send a decent amount back home. They enjoy the lifestyle in East London, where there is a strong Asian community. Some of the men don't have any intentions of going back to Pakistan any time soon; they have already spoken to the college owner to get themselves enrolled in another course when their MBA is completed.

 Kashif puts his hand luggage in the cabin space above his seat; he then sits down and immediately opens his book — *The Alchemist* by Paolo Coelho. He feels nervous, not so much because he is travelling for the first time completely on his own but because people on board have still not been settled. He anticipates all sorts of different things that make him nervous: whether he needs to say hello to the middle-aged woman sat next to him, laden with gold and holding tightly onto her bag, whether someone might move his bag and jacket, neatly placed in the cabin luggage compartment or would someone come and tell him that he has sat on the wrong seat. He looks at his boarding card and checks again — 16D. "This is 16D for sure," he murmurs to himself. He then tries hard to keep his focus on the book. Fortunately, in a matter of minutes, everything seemed to have settled without causing him any disturbance and the captain informs the cabin crew that the plane is ready to take off.

Kashif closes his eyes and begins to recollect his life spent in Pakistan. The first image that forces its way into his mind is the memory of his first day at his new primary school. He recalls how, when he joined the new school in the second grade as oppose to first which is the norm, he had trouble making his way into the alien environment as the rest of the boys were already friends with each other. He remembers distinctly the first day in the new school. It was already very hard for Kashif to make any friends but when the school finished it was raining down very heavily. It was a total chaos, with kids running around and outside the premises. Kashif struggled to find his way out and when he eventually did, he got lost outside the premises. He took the wrong exit gate and his school bus was at the other gate. As an eight-year-old at that time, Kashif began to cry in panic and then was eventually helped by two senior students who took him to his van. It had made Kashif very anxious and fair to say that he lost his confidence to go to that new school. That began an era for him where he was too scared to go to school and started making all sorts of ridiculous excuses every day to avoid school. His parents persevered and, like it or not, Kashif was dragged to attend the school. Then one day, things took a turn for better. The appointment of the new teacher for English literature was to be decisive in

Kashif's motivation for school and generally in life. She was young, caring and beautiful. Kashif had an immediate crush on this elegant, petite fair-skinned teacher. The teacher was clever and she used this situation to bring the best out in him. Kashif started to look forward to going to school, making sure his uniform is tidy and all his homework is complete. The teacher asked him to perform well in every subject, not just in English, and make more friends, participate in sports and other extra-curricular activities. Kashif came second in the overall ranking for his second grade. He progressed through grades and was recognised as a top student with versatile talents especially in cricket and elocution. The teacher became his mentor and one day, when Kashif was in the sixth grade, she invited him to the staff room and informed him that she is leaving the school. She is about to get married and move to the United States with her husband. Kashif was visibly upset but she made him promise to continue his efforts, be successful and one day marry a beautiful girl. Later on, she gave Kashif a goodbye card which Kashif has still kept with him. In fact, it is in the book that he is reading now. Kashif then pulls out the card from the back of his book given to him by his English teacher, which contained an excerpt from the Irish Blessing:

Dearest Kashif,

May you have enough happiness to keep you sweet, enough trials to keep you strong, enough sorrow to keep you human, enough hope to keep you happy, enough failure to keep you humble, enough success to keep you eager, enough friends to give you comfort, enough faith and courage in yourself to banish sadness, enough wealth to meet your needs and one thing more — enough determination to make each day a more wonderful day than the one before.

And remember that you will always be in my best wishes!
Yours Sincerely,
Miss Farzana

He smiles and takes a long hard look at the card and imagines her beautiful face. He remembers her last day at school when she sent for him to meet her in the library. How the sunlight creeping through the sun blinds fell on her face and she looked divine in her white and green dress. How he trembled inside with the immense enchantment when he was confronted by her aura. He could barely remember what she said to him but he knew that whatever she said, she meant it. He remembers how he was unable to utter a single word or make sense out of the situation. His face turned long and he look down on the floor, knowing that he possibly won't see her again. She then gives him a goodbye card and Kashif just holds it and continues to look sadly towards the floor. When she asked him if he is going to open the card in front of her, he shook his head sideways and said, with no hesitation, that he will miss her. She was touched and gave him a strong hug. She asked him to promise her that he will work hard to achieve whatever he wants to in life and Kashif promised. The hug calmed his nerves down and he was able to breathe, having been accepted by the aura of this wonderful woman.

"What brings you to the United Kingdom, sir?"

"I'm here to forget my past and create a future for myself, ma'am"

The immigration officer sat on a raised chair smiles but keeps her eyes on Kashif's passport while she searches for his

UK visa. "And how do you plan to go about creating a future for yourself in the UK, sir?"

"I am enrolled to study for my master's degree in robotics at King's College London, ma'am."

The visa officer, having found a valid student's visa on Kashif's passport, this time turns towards Kashif. "Can I see your acceptance letter from the university and your residence agreement please?"

Kashif, being organised and proactive by nature, brings the documents out immediately. "There you go, ma'am..."

She then asks Kashif to put his right thumb and then all four of his right-hand fingers, one by one, on the fingerprint reader and records the biometrics information.

"Where are you heading to after this, sir?"

"I am heading straight to the King's College dorms at West Hampstead, ma'am."

Knowing the questionable ways in which Faisal and his friends live, Kashif decides not to mention anything about his East London dwelling to be to the visa officer. She then asks Kashif to fill out the landing card with all the information and confidently stamps Kashif's visa with the Heathrow Airport entry stamp.

"Off you go, sir. All the best!"

Faisal, a tall dark and handsome-looking man with gelled spiked hair and a shiny ear stud, waits outside the arrival gate. He is moving his head to the Punjabi tunes he has put on his shiny blue iPod Nano. He is wearing skin-tight blue denim jeans, expensive Nike Air Max trainers and a blue Adidas jacket with white stripes. He sees a confused-looking Kashif coming out of the arrival gate trying to look for his mate.

Faisal, being mischievous, enjoys the moment and lets Kashif sweat a little before sneaking up to him.

"Freshy!"

Faisal uses this term, which is used to describe new people coming from the Asian subcontinent, endearingly to greet Kashif. He then immediately puts his arms around Kashif and gives him a strong hug. Kashif does the same.

"I'm really sorry about Uncle Zaidi's death, Kashif."

Kashif nods his head and then hugs Faisal again.

"Let's take you home, partner," Faisal says in an energetic voice, trying to shed off the sadness that they both feel.

He lends Kashif a spare oyster card and teaches him everything he needs to know about the London Underground. Helping Kashif with his luggage, the boys travel on the Piccadilly line towards London. Faisal takes Kashif through the tube map and explains to him that they will need to swap to Central line and then get off at Stratford Station. Then they talk about everything: from the death of Kashif's father to Faisal's love life, about the personalities and habits of Kashif's housemates to be. Faisal tells Kashif that he has already lined up a job interview for him, the next afternoon, as a cashier at Sainsbury's. Kashif feels at home in London already, although he seems out of touch with the fashion in London, speaks very much in an Indian accent and looks at women in the tube with so much excitement as if he has never seen one before. Faisal puts his music on and gives one earphone to Kashif and wears the other one himself. They listen to Faisal's mixed playlist of UK and Punjabi music while Kashif continues to sneak a glance or two at the women around him while trying to comprehend the tube map that his friend gave him.

When Kashif arrives at his new Glen Park Road house, he is surprised to see how clean the house is inside, even though they are five other men living in it. It is only Faisal's elder brother who is at the house while the rest are at the local cinema at the other end of Green Street to watch the new Indian movie. Faisal shows Kashif his room that he will now share with himself and his brother. The three men then sit down to have dinner — minced lamb meat, rice and vegetable stew — cooked by Faisal's brother. The food is very nicely cooked and Kashif indulges himself freely into it. The boys get talking after the dinner. Both Faisal and his brother are interested in the developments and the gossip back home in Karachi, Pakistan. They enjoy being a little nostalgic and then Kashif excuses himself as sleep overcomes him. Faisal makes sure that Kashif is settled in the room and shows him the side of the bed that he will be sleeping and that Faisal will sleep next to Kashif while Faisal's brother sleeps on the sofa-bed.

The next morning, Kashif is able to meet all the rest of the members of the household. The meeting is brief as the men are off to work in a supermarket. They seem happy to meet Kashif for many reasons: they now have a sixth member in their house, meaning the bills will be divided equally and also Kashif, being clever, good-looking and fluent in English, should prove a useful asset and someone they could feel proud to hang around with in London. They wish Kashif best of luck as Faisal's plan is to take Kashif to Sainsbury's near Holborn in central London, in the next hour, for an informal interview for the post of a sales assistant. They have a quick cup of coffee with fruit and nut mix cereals. On the way, Faisal decides to brief Kashif on the basics of customer services techniques. He also tells him how to please the store manager, Hayley — a tall good-looking blonde with short hair who likes dark men — by smiling at her and looking her in the eye while speaking to her. He also tips Kashif to be sure to compliment Hayley on the cleanliness and orderliness that in the store.

The boys take two trains from their East London house and arrive at the store at quarter to eleven, which is fifteen minutes before the start of Faisal's shift. Faisal takes Kashif with him to the store manager's office and she is expecting them. The store manager, who is twenty-seven but looks about twenty, immediately takes a liking to Kashif. Kashif's big hazel eyes, curved eyelashes and charming smile are enough to get her pupils dilated. She asks Kashif a couple of basic questions about where he studies and does he have a valid visa — more in a way of gaining acquaintance as opposed to a formal job interview.

Faisal, being a proud friend, immediately jumps in. "He is a very intelligent cookie, Hayley. He'll be studying at King's College! He only arrived yesterday."

Hayley nods her head and then thanks Faisal for bringing Kashif along and tells him politely that he should get ready for his shift. She then asks Kashif to come back at two p.m. when she finishes her shift so that she could interview him in more detail. Kashif agrees and sees this as his first opportunity to explore London; he needs to kill about three hours before he returns to the store. To his surprise, Haley herself very kindly suggests to him that while he is in the area, he should go and look at the King's College Strand Campus, then visit the impeccable Maughan Library on Chancery Lane and then, if he fancies, he could take the long walk to St. Paul's Cathedral and then back here. All of this being at walking distance from the store. She then prints out a map for Kashif from her office computer, circles these places and hands it over to Kashif. Kashif thanks Hayley and she gives the handsome young man an extended smile, showing signs of interest. Kashif smiles back flirtatiously and excuses himself out of the premises, being sure that he has landed his first job in the city of London.

9

"Who among you can drive a truck? I need two volunteers for our next mission."

Almost every recruit raises their hands in response to Uthman's question. Adnan also joins in with the herd, even though he has never driven a truck before and once or twice his brother's car. He only knows how to drive his Yamaha 100cc two-stroke motorbike. However, Adnan, like the rest of the recruits, is so eager to get onboard with this unknown, unspoken mission that he is happy to lie to Uthman about his driving abilities. He tries desperately to make eye contact with Uthman while holding his hand up in hope that he would somehow convince him, or at least be able to show his eagerness for being a part of this activity.

Uthman has kept a close eye on Adnan since the day he came to see him regarding his dream. He has witnessed, over the past few days, how eager Adnan is to please him. And not only that; Adnan has shown great strength and agility during the Mujahideen training. This is exactly the kind of attitude that Uthman is looking for in his recruits before trusting them with any task or any other serious mission. He has also had feedback on the driving abilities of some of the recruits and one of them stands out. So, effectively, Uthman had already made the choice of the two recruits he wants to send on the mission; Adnan and Dawar. The former because of his enthusiasm and commitment the latter because of his calmness and impressive driving skills.

"I have been watching you all closely and so are my comrades. You all have done brilliantly so far and I'm sure you will continue to impress Allah and his Prophet with the same dedication to the jihadi cause. Rest assured, all of you will be serving Allah one way or the other and some of you may need to wait for the right task for you. So please do not be impatient and, more importantly, never be disappointed. For this little task I have chosen our brother Dawar to be the driver of the truck and our brother Adnan to assist him. Congratulations to the two of you!" Uthman finds the two recruits who are stood a fair distance apart inside the makeshift mosque where he is addressing the recruits and gives them a smile. The boys smile back with pride gleaming through their eyes. Uthman continues, "You might be taking a truck for a long drive so make sure you pack all your belongings tonight and meet us here tomorrow morning nine a.m. sharp. And no more training for you two — it is time now to put some of the lessons learned into actions!"

The boys, without any question, agree and decide between themselves to be at the mosque by eight thirty a.m. instead, to avoid any last-minute chaos. As they are now excused from the daily Mujahideen training, they have nothing else to do. Hence, they just need to pack their luggage which will only take them about an hour at most.

The boys arrive at the mosque on time, looking and feeling very happy, even though they well understand that this mission could lead to their death and that it could be a suicide mission. Still, they are excited about it without any fear of death.

Adnan says to his new chosen partner, Dawar, who has unusually smooth skin for twenty-four-year-old and virtually no facial hair, "I am so happy that you are with me on this mission. Not that I am scared to go alone but it feels good to have someone who shares the same excitement as I do. I don't know what the mission is going to be but I know that there is a chance that you and I won't come out alive. Are you scared about that?"

Dawar shakes his head and blinks his eyes slowly, suggesting that he is not scared, and continues to read over his prayer bread.

Adnan continues, "You know, Dawar, of all the battles that a man fights, the biggest is the one within. Right now I am struggling to keep my focus — my mind is constantly thinking about my family, my mom's chicken biryani, me playing cricket on the streets and then riding on my motorbike at night, along with my friends, to drink chai and eat paratha from the famous Gulberg chai shop. But then I need to remind myself that this is not how Allah wants me to spend my limited days on his earth. My days are best spent in submission to Allah's will and his commands. I have to fight my personal desires to put his will above everything else. And once I have done that, then only the heaven with its seventy-two virgins awaits me!

"And what better death can there be than that of a martyr? Alhamdulillah! I simply cannot wait for this experience that is about to start. See already and how swiftly the Almighty has taken away my mind from thinking about the daily pleasure and frivolous things in life! Subhan Allah! Now, I crave to feel my sweet transformation from this meaningless world to the heaven above. I can imagine myself passing through the skies, being carried on by angels, so beautiful that I can spend the eternity admiring their beauty. Walking through the lush green fields of heaven that consists of flowing rivers of pure white milk, crystal clear water, wine and sweet honey. A selection of fine horses is available for me to pick. I choose a white horse and ride on him through the beautiful sea of green. Then I stop by at a farm, where, near a cosy little hut surrounded by red tulips, one of my beautiful virgins is working in the fields. Her skin is whiter than milk, her eyes are blue as water and her hair, shining like sunlight. I kiss her soft juicy pink lips and we make love under the tree for hours. Tired after that, we drink wine from the river and feast on the food which angels will serve us. Ah! All of this awaits us, my brother! Isn't that great?"

This time, the smooth-skinned Dawar gives Adnan a warm genuine smile and says, "Yes — Allah is great indeed! And like you, Adnan, I also cannot wait to be in heaven and leave this filthy world behind me! I have been bad for a good part of my life, Adnan. I cannot thank Allah enough that he has given me this opportunity to redeem myself. I bow down to his might and surrender myself to his mercy and benevolence. I swear, Adnan, on my life, that before tasting the sacred wine from heaven, I will kill as many idol worshippers as I can in Allah's name. I will prove myself worthy of being chosen by Allah for this mission. And you, Adnan, are my true friend, as we are both chosen by the almighty to serve his just cause and may Allah grant us martyrdom! Amen."

"Amen!" Adnan seconds the other recruit's emotions.

Uthman arrives at 9 a.m. sharp with a tall, middle-aged guy who is clean-shaven, both from his head and beard. The guy is wearing worn-out black jeans which appear to have lost colour, especially around the thigh area, due to frequent washing. Uthman introduces this reasonably urban-looking guy to the two recruits and asks them to call him Ustad, meaning 'the teacher' in Urdu. Ustad, who has a very deep voice, a slim figure and a fair complexion, hands both of them a relatively large shopping bag. The bag contains a pair of new blue jeans, used but clean white and black V-neck t-shirt and a pair of used black boots with socks. He instructs the boys to change into their new clothes. Once again, both the recruits, without asking any questions, change into the Western clothes and put their shalwar-kameez, the traditional Pakistani dresses, in the same bag. The attire fits the boys perfectly.

"Ustad will first take you to the barber who will give you a modern haircut and a decent trim on your beards. This is very important as we would want you to disguise yourselves as moderate Muslims or even Westerners. With your looks you might be mistaken as Bollywood dancing extras in a film! Or just wannabees! The less the Indians suspect you, the easier it will be to execute the mission. And do not worry — Allah understands that you will shave your beards and wear Western clothes for a bigger cause. After the haircut, you will be taken to Srinagar, not via crawling through the tunnel this time but will be driven in a car. Ustad will take photos of you and attach them to your new Indian passports, having all your details already printed with your existing names. You are not to lose your passports under any circumstance. You are also to practice your signatures as Ustad has scribed on your passports. Then comes the main bit. In Srinagar, you will work as helpers in the kitchen of a restaurant owned by an old Sikh friend of ours called Pa Jee. Pa Jee's heart is with the Muslims of Kashmir plus he is anti-Hindu. Pa Jee's innocent brother and father were brutally killed in front of him by the Indian nationalist mob during the 1984 anti-Sikh riots in India after the assassination of the Indian prime minister, Indra Gandhi, by her two Sikh bodyguards. Pa Jee was only a little boy at that time. He tells us about the horrors of those days when the Hindus took to the streets of India to kill the Sikhs in order to avenge Indra Gandhi's death. Her bodyguards killed her after she sanctioned the Operation Blue Star. The operation gave an open license to the police to capture, torture or kill Sikhs who sought independence from India to form an independent Sikh state called 'Khalistan'. Pa Jee and his family have always been huge supporters of the Khalistan movement. Pa Jee still sheds a tear or two when he recollects how the Indian police and the army just stood there and watched his father and brother being kicked and battered to death by the mob. His hatred for the Indians is deeply rooted and he will do anything to inflict misery on the Indian army. This makes Pa Jee our ally so it is important for you to know why he is supporting us. Now, the most important thing for you to remember is never to speak to anyone else apart from Pa Jee and Ustad from now on unless it is simple acknowledgement or related to activities of the restaurant. Nothing about me, your personal lives, where you come from and specially about 'The Army of Muhammad'. Is it understood?"

"Yes, caliph!" The boys reply with a sense of pride and excitement in their voice.

Uthman continues, "You will start working in Pa Jee's kitchen from tonight and it will only be in the evenings. During the morning, Ustad will prepare you for the mission ahead. I will come to see you in a week's time and stay with you until the mission is accomplished. Do you have any questions?"

The boys look at each other and then reply, "No, caliph!"

"Fine — then may Allah keep you in his guard." Uthman kisses the recruits on their forehead and signals Ustad to take them. The boys feel excited as they feel that they are now fully on board with the mission.

The boys put their luggage in the boot of Ustad's car — a white Toyota Corolla registered under 1994 number plates and in top condition. With the air conditioning on full blow and recital of the Quran by the Imam of Mecca playing loudly on the stereo, they head out. Adnan looks outside the back-seat window; the sun is shining hot and there are a few people walking about the streets, going about their business. His eyes briefly stop at a dog, sitting next to a patch of grass, panting and looking towards them. Adnan wonders why the dog is not sitting in the shade. 'The dog knows and is laughing with joy that God's will is about to be fulfilled', he thinks… The car stops at a very small barber shop with only a single barber chair inside. The barber comes out immediately to greet Ustad as if he was waiting for him to arrive for some time. Adnan takes the barber's chair first. The barber uses number two clippers around the sides and the back of Adnan's head and trims the rest of his silky black hair with regular scissors. He then changes the number to one and pushes the clippers down Adnan cheeks and trims his beard to a length that gives a look that he hasn't shaved for only a day but by no means can anyone tell that he had previously kept a full-size beard. After the trims, that only took forty-five minutes altogether, both the boys look like extras for a Bollywood movie — exactly as Uthman had predicted! No one can tell their religious extremism pedigree now.

Ustad then drives them to their house where they will stay for the time the mission is accomplished. The drive is long but comfortable; Adnan falls asleep in the back seat while the smooth-skinned stays vigilant as if he is anticipating orders from Ustad to attack the Indian army any minute. Ustad is naturally quiet and extremely shy. He does not utter a single word during the journey and neither is he interested in knowing anything about the boys or asking them any questions. Little is known about Ustad himself and the jobs he undertakes as a Pakistani CIA agent. Maintaining a healthy relationship between both the Mujahideen and the Pakistan army, at the same time, takes its toll on him as a CIA agent. He has to ensure that the Mujahideen get their drug money safely without any media or public attention and also that the Pakistan army is seen to be cutting down on the Mujahideen. The latter task is the most difficult for him. He has achieved this to a certain level by killing the criminals who are arrested on murder charges by Pakistan police or CIA themselves. Most of these criminals are from remote villages without any identification and haven't yet faced a state trial. Ustad and his CIA colleagues also ensure that the criminals have no family and friends resourceful enough to come out looking for them and causing him or his colleagues any grief later on. He had provided these criminals local clothes — shalwar kameez to wear instead of the prison uniform and told them not to shave in order to have a beard. All this because the CIA wants these unproved criminals to look like Mujahideens. Ustad, along with his CIA mates, would then take them to a remote valley somewhere in the north and ask them to run away. They then shoot them from behind and then, after ensuring that they are dead, place AK 47s in their hands or near them. They make it look like these men were Mujahideen, killed while trying to escape when encountered by the Pakistan army or CIA. Ustad would then take pictures of these dead bodies with the Pakistan army present. Sometimes, to make it look different and keep monotony away from the press, they take these prisoners, handcuffed, to a remote empty hut and place them in different rooms and then shoot them at point blank range. They even put a Pakistan army uniform on some and give them a shave to make it look like a gun battle, making it look more realistic, and show that the Pakistan army has also had their losses. Apart from all this, Ustad and the CIA also need to ensure that none of the Mujahideen get involved in civilian politics or commit crimes against the Pakistani civilians. It is indeed a very tough job, hence he has become quieter and withdrawn over time.

    The boys have reached their house. It is about a mile away from the Indian army headquarter that they had previously seen with Uthman when they came through the tunnel. From the roof of the house, one can easily see the headquarters exact location and appearance. Adnan is woken up from his snooze feeling fresh but, by now, smooth-skinned Dawar is feeling slightly tired. The house is a pale-green coloured two-storey building. The ground floor is made into an automotive garage and upstairs are the kitchen and two en suite rooms, which are being used as bedrooms. Without wasting any time, Ustad turns the padlock keys and lifts the shutter gates of the garage and takes the two boys inside.

The garage walls, even though painted white, appear grey because of dirt. It is evident that the house isn't being looked after. However, the boys see an old silver Mazda 808 parked in the front and behind it is an old but nicely decorated, yellow Hinopak truck, both in nice clean condition. Ustad has told the boys to leave their luggage behind in the car and follow him to the garage. Ustad than takes out three bottles of Pepsi from the small white fridge in the corner and offers one each to the boys. They all drink together; Ustad then asks the boys to hop onto the truck and asks Dawar to take the driver's seat and reverse the truck out from the back door while he and Adnan sit next to him. Dawar is able to perform the manoeuvre with ease. Ustad then asks him to drive on the road slowly. Dawar follows the instructions to the letter and Ustad seems pleased. They bring the truck back to the garage and Ustad, with brevity, says to the boys, "Well done, smooth-skinned! You will be the driver of the truck and Adnan — you will help him in this mission. Now get your bags from the car and I'll show you your room."

He then takes them to their room, which has two separate single beds each equipped with a single pillow and a thin quilt. The walls have lost paint but patches of white paint can still be seen. There is a calligraphic picture saying Allah on the side wall. There is one decent-size window with a thick blue curtain on the opposite side of the entrance door and a hanging light bulb in the centre. "I will come and pick you up at six p.m. sharp. Keep these clothes on and I'll take you guys to Pa Jee".

Ustad then leaves the boys inside the room and calls Uthman from his mobile phone while walking towards his car. "The first boy I tried was the smooth-skinned and he is an excellent driver! And Adnan, your favourite — we know already very well that he is keen. I don't think that they need weeks of training for this! I think they are ready!"

Uthman takes a moment and then replies, "Hmm, OK, take them to the Sikh as planned tonight and I'll make my way now and meet you guys there."

Ustad replies, "OK. Khuda Hafiz" and puts the phone down.

10

The Healthy Gym is located on the second floor of a newly constructed building. On the ground and the first floor beneath the gym is a restaurant that serves grilled chicken, lamb meat with paratha and mint yoghurt. It is a very famous restaurant among the locals; in fact, the entire area surrounding the Healthy Gym is very busy. During the day it is busy mainly because of the money exchange, banks, electronics and home fittings shops bringing different customers. Then, as soon as evening falls, the place attracts lots of young men because of the gym plus families for food. There are other little kiosks that remain open from the middle of the day till late at night and they sell milk shakes, home-made burgers and mobile phone accessories. The area is also famous because of a skilled electrician who has developed a reputation for fixing and unlocking any make of mobile phones. Some people come to him with stolen mobile phones that he buys off them and re-sells at a higher price. Others, who live mostly abroad, bring him mobile phones to unlock which they usually have obtained by making false insurance claims. This makes up for a perfect expensive gift for their loved ones in Karachi and costs them almost nothing; just a few lies to the insurance company and a cover-up story.

  Layla arrives at the gym during the women-only hours i.e. between eleven a.m. and four p.m. At the reception desk,

Siddiq is sat visibly engrossed in solving the past exam papers of physics for his tenth-grade exams. Layla finds it surprising that a young boy, handsomely built with a geeky but an attractive face, is allowed at the reception during the women-only timing. But Siddiq does not show any signs of interest in women coming in and out of the gym — he is focused completely at his work since his mock matriculation exams are round the corner. He took the job as he has a three-week study break and could always do with some extra cash. The gym is owned by one of his family members, so getting the job at the reception was never really a problem for him. Also, he is extra careful in not getting involved with the women attending the gym to avoid any kind of disrepute he may bring to his so-called family gym.

"I want to renew my membership and I have lost my card. I have been away for a few months; I just had a baby boy! Pregnancy has made me very fat! As you can see…" Layla puts her hand bag on the reception table, which is just about her chest height, and leans forward to get an eye contact with Siddiq who keeps his head down but only lifts his eyes to see her. He immediately feels his heart race as his eyes meets Layla's. Although she has spent very little time curling her eye lashes with mascara, she is a woman of fine and attractive features; it proves enough to race the heartbeat of young Siddiq.

"The system is down today, ma'am, and will not be fixed until six p.m. today, when the owner comes in. So you'll need to come again tomorrow to get your membership renewed — I'm sorry. And by the way, you are not fat!" Siddiq checks himself, fearing he might have spoken more than he was supposed to and immediately turns his gaze back towards his book.

Layla smiles at the compliment but intent on getting her workout routine going, she argues, "Thank you, young man, for your nice words! However, it is not my fault that your system is down you see, so please take the money and give it to your boss and he can issue me the card later, whenever he is back. This way, I can use the gym today and collect the card tomorrow. I can trust you with my money I think — you seem like an honest young man. What are you studying?"

"Physics." Siddiq feels that he cannot argue back against Layla's charm and her intelligent suggestion. "And he is not my boss — the owner. I'm his cousin and working here part-time for some extra pocket money."

"Good for you then, young man! How old are you?"

"Twenty." Siddiq finds himself inadvertently lying about his age in order to impress Layla. He feels as if he has already broken the unspoken code and is now flirting with this gorgeous woman.

"Don't lie trying to impress me, young man. The matriculation course book hasn't changed in years and you don't seem like a boy who would fail a grade. So, sixteen?" Layla puts the question back.

"You are very clever," Siddiq complements Layla with a smile. "I'm eighteen though and yes, I haven't failed any of my grades but I started school late as I spent a couple of years learning the Quran by heart."

"Well done! Now is the membership still five hundred rupees?"

"Yes." Siddiq has agreed to Layla's earlier suggestion without saying it out loud.

"There you go then." Layla hands him over the money. "I need a locker key."

"But you need to fill in the form first. I believe it is here somewhere!" Siddiq tries to look for the membership form but struggles to find it. Layla shows her impatience and appears unimpressed by taking a deep sigh. "Never mind, if you could please write your name, telephone number and address then I'll sort it out for you."

Layla obliges immediately, as she cannot wait to get on the treadmill and lose the extra belly fat.

"Thank you. My name is Siddiq, by the way, and I'll make sure that your membership is sorted today and you can collect the card from me tomorrow. I'll be working here during women-only hours." Siddiq smiles, and with a hesitant voice, asks Layla, "Do you want me to show you around?"

"I was a member here before — remember I told you! Now you should focus back on your books, young man, and thank you very much." Layla smiles back and collects her bag.

"Sure." Siddiq feels that he's been put back in his place and focuses back onto his book.

Layla climbs up the stairs and feels happy about the fact that she has still got what it takes to captivate even young men by her beauty and intelligence.

It has been almost a month since the death of Dr. Zaidi and about a week since Kashif, his son, has moved to London. Layla has regained her lithe figure after the pregnancy by working hard on the treadmill and in her Pilates class. She has converted her little flirtatious encounters with Siddiq into more of a closer bond by asking him to tuition her little daughter in the first grade for a meagre fee of five hundred rupees a month. Siddiq agreed as it was a perfect opportunity for him to stay close to Layla; she has been in his imagination ever since he met her. Sometimes the imagination becomes so strong, distracting him from his studies, that Siddiq finds himself masturbating, picturing Layla in his mind. This hasn't solved anything but instead Siddiq finds himself masturbating twice or even thrice every day. Siddiq will start teaching Layla's daughter once he has finished his mock exams in a couple of weeks' time.

Layla has always been conscious of Madiha's fair-skinned high-cheekbone beautiful face. She is, to a certain extent, jealous of Madiha. Omar has always reacted strangely, almost nervously, whenever they meet Madiha and that did not help Layla's feelings towards her. Hence the reason she took this long to get herself back in shape first before meeting Madiha. Omar and Layla arrive at Dr. Zaidi's house. It is an early February Sunday evening; winter has decided to stay longer in Karachi this year. The street outside Dr. Zaidi's house, which is usually full of children playing cricket outside, is quiet, as it gets dark early in winter. Madiha is alone in the house and she lets the couple in as Omar rings the intercom bell. Madiha knew that they were coming — Omar had texted her. Before her son, Kashif, left for London, Omar had helped him buy a leather jacket from one of his friend's shop. In fact, Omar paid for it too. Kashif had told Omar that he'll leave his mobile phone behind with Madiha when he leaves for England. And since Kashif left, Omar had been texting Madiha daily to inquire how she is and if she needs anything. At first,

Madiha didn't reply so Omar stopped, thinking that she is taking her time and then eventually, after a couple of days, she began to respond. As always, Madiha is very simple in her dressing today and wears a plain navy-blue shalwar kameez with a white dupatta. She has let her hair down and has put a mild red color lipstick, just enough not make her lips prominent but very kissable. She opens the drawing room door to the couple and greets them warmly with a smile.

"I'm so happy to see you, Layla. Congratulations on the new born." Madiha's eyes shone when spoke to Layla. She held Layla's hand and kept smiling at her, trying her best not to let the pain of her husband's recent death show. It does the trick; Layla loses the script from her mind that she had been preparing all the way in the car. It appears to Layla that offering condolences might sombre the mood and wipe the smile off Madiha's face.

So Layla plays it by ear, and replies warmly and with a voice that matches Madiha's intensity, almost taking the tone of a very close friend, "Thank you so much, Madiha — he is already our bundle of joy!"

"How is Kashif? He must be loving London! I would love to go there one day!" Both Layla and Madiha take the two-seater sofa and sit sideways, facing next to each other. Omar takes the seat next to Layla that faces towards the two women. Layla has her back towards Omar but he can very well see Madiha's delicate face and elegant body facing him.

"I spoke with him today; he is happy. He says that there is no excuse for anyone to be bored in London as there is always something happening. He has also found a job there, thanks to the grace of the Almighty!" Madiha replies, with a promising smile on her face, and looks at Omar while keeping her smile.

"I'm so happy for him. He is a good kid. Both Layla and I always liked him. I'm sure he will do great in London," Omar replies, with a promising smile on his face.

Layla, sensing the flirtatious rhythm between her husband and Madiha, tries to hastily fill the silence. "Indeed, Kashif is a very rational kid; I have never seen him act on emotions since I have known him. But that makes me wonder whether he took his time to really grieve his father's death. I mean, was he in the right frame of mind when he went to London, as it was very soon after Dr. Zaidi's death?"

Madiha looks at Layla for a few seconds longer after Layla has spoken. Instead of replying, she drops her gaze and thinks about changing the topic. She understands the point Layla makes here. Kashif has always kept his worries to himself. She remembers well, during Kashif's primary school days, that for almost a month he did not answer her when she asked him if he had eaten his lunch. He would act normal and just say, 'Mom, you can check my lunch box'. It wasn't until one day, during the lunch break, she went to Kashif's school to pay the fees that she figured out what had been happening. Two older boys would come to Kashif and his two other friends and take the goodies from their lunch boxes, leaving them with just the sandwiches. Kashif and his friends would not retaliate against these bullies but would continue to eat their sandwiches as if nothing had happened. Madiha remembers going up to the bullies and making them return those goodies to her kids and his friends. Since then Kashif began to give Madiha the normal answer of 'Yes, Mom' back whenever she asked him about his lunch.

"Why would you bring up Dr. Zaidi's death, Layla? Madiha and Kashif are trying to move on here, I believe. Kashif has gone to King's College London to fulfil his father's wishes. I think both Madiha and Kashif have channelled their emotions into actions that the late Dr. Zaidi would be proud of!" The words came out of Omar's mouth with uncharacteristic coldness that is now being felt in the room. There is a pin-drop silence. Layla conceals her anger towards her husband; she does not want Madiha to see that she is upset. Omar questioning her like this is in front of another person is something that Layla has never experienced before. Omar, on the other hand, immediately regrets these words and screams inside to himself, 'Why the fuck did I not stay quiet'?

Madiha keeps her calm and, with her gaze still down towards the floor, breaks the silence. "I'll fetch you guys some tea."

Not a single word is being spoken between Omar and Layla even though Madiha has left them to go to the kitchen. Not even during their way home in the car and until they go to bed. What has upset Layla the most is that her husband has defended someone else instead of her — something that he has never done before since the day she had met him. 'Clearly, that bitch has casted a spell on Omar! Now that she is single, she will show herself available to other men. Omar always fancied her — that I knew — but to see him defend that bitch against me is something that I never imagined'! Layla obsesses about these thoughts in her head; soon she could hear Omar snore in his sleep next to her.

11

Ustad does not knock on the boys' bedroom door but instead barges in at five minutes to six. Why would he knock? After all, he owns this place and it is also the best way to know whether the boys are ready for the task or not.
Sneaking up to them and catching them off-guard seemed like a part of the plan. To Ustad's comfort, both the boys are neatly dressed with their bags packed and they have an eager look on their faces. "There has been a change of plan," Ustad authoritatively tells the boys after exchanging greetings. "Uthman is coming to Pa Jee's restaurant tonight to brief you on your first mission. Now, because of commitment throughout the Mujahideen camp and the eagerness you have shown, both Uthman and myself think that you are ready for this mission. So we will not train you in isolation any further, but instead, put you on the ground with Pa Jee straightaway. There you will learn the basics of waiter skills and we will finalise the details of the mission quickly. So you don't need days of training and will soon receive details of the mission. Now I ask you, are you ready for it? Are you ready to fulfil your promise to Allah and do jihad for him?"

Both Adnan and Smooth Skin replied without any hesitation, "Allah hu Akbar!"

They arrive shortly at Pa Jee's restaurant. It is an open-spaced restaurant without any conventional entrance doors; it is made by breaking the walls between two shops and has a huge metal shutter in the front that can easily be closed if there are any disturbances outside. The restaurant is well lit with white light. It has tables next to each other while people are free to move both the chairs and tables around to suit their numbers. The tiled floor towards the left corner of the restaurant is elevated in the form of an L-shape. At the front, above the shorter end of the L-shape, there is a giant and extremely hot barbecue grill with naked chickens hanging from the metal bar attached to the ceiling. Towards the longer end of the L-shaped elevation there are three big cauldrons, also very hot and on a high flame generated through burning coal. The first contains *nihari* which is the national dish of Pakistan — a South Asian curry made of slow-cooked beef along with bone marrow — tastes much like the Hungarian dish, goulash. The second caldron is filled with *haleem* — a famous Middle Eastern stew made of wheat, barley, lentils and beef. And the final cauldron holds a spicy chicken biryani. The person sat behind the L-shape elevated space on a high chair is a huge larger-than-life man called Pa Jee. Although in his early thirties, Pa Jee looks much older as if he has aged twice with every single breath. Pa Jee is an Indian Sikh trusted by Jaish-e-Muhammad and acts as a spy for them. Both Adnan and smooth-skinned have come to stay with Pa Jee under disguise until their mission is complete. He wears a dark-blue turban and a white shalwar kameez; his big black eyes and curved eyelashes are still his most prominent facial features even though he has a huge black beard.

"Salaam, Pa Jee!" Ustad shouts loud enough to get Pa Jee's attention as he is busy turning the barbecue chicken kebabs on the grille. "I have here with me Adnan and smooth-skinned for you; the boys that you requested to help you with your chores in the restaurant. These two strong boys are here to do exactly that! They are young, fit and eager to please; I am sure that you will welcome them with an open heart." Ustad smiles cleverly after saying these words.

Pa Jee smiles back to Ustad with his eyes gleaming in agreement of what has just been spoken to him. Pa Jee asks one of his men to take the three guests inside his office at the back of the restaurant. Adnan takes a quick glance at the *nihari* in the caldron — his favourite. The look and smell of the spicy beef has brought water in his mouth.

"Don't worry, young man, I'll send the food inside for all of you." Pa Jee, spotting Adnan almost drooling from his mouth, says this warmly to him. Adnan smiles back. Forget worrying about the first impression of meeting his new employer or let alone the mission — Adnan is now looking forward to getting his hand on the *nihari* with naan bread.

As soon as the men settle down around an oval shaped table in the office, used mainly to sit together and dine, Pa Jee walks in the room with Uthman and another man. That was much to everyone's surprise. Uthman has also brought an Indian man of large build with him — darkest among all the men in the room and with very distinctive smiling eyes. Uthman hangs his turban and his machine gun on the coat hangers of the wall. He then takes the seat next to Ustad opposite the two boys. Pa Jee sits next to the boys while the Indian man stands next to Uthman, as they are only five chairs among the six men.

"I heard that you both have done really well today. Especially you, smooth-skinned; you seem to be an expert in handling the truck. Adnan, I know that you are Allah's angel who is always willing to serve him with complete devotion." Uthman addresses the boys with an encouraging smile on his face. Both the boys have worked hard in the training camps but have never received direct praise from Uthman. Now, rightly so, they both feel flattered to receive praise from Uthman as they see him as their leader and a caliph; direct praise from him is akin to being praised by the Prophet Muhammad himself.

"The time has come, my brothers, to surrender your worldly lives completely in order to live eternally. Think of yourselves as martyrs now. Think of yourselves flying through the seven clouds and carried by angels to your palaces of eternal abode. Think of yourself drinking milk from the golden chalice and that milk being poured by the Prophet Muhammad himself. Think of yourself meeting your seventy-two virgins and having coitus with them for as long as you like. For tomorrow will be the day when you will receive what every soldier of Allah has dreamed of; tomorrow you will be his martyrs. Do you have any fear?"

The boys take a moment before replying together almost in perfect chorus, "No."

Uthman senses nervousness among the boys — he is a clever fox. It is certainly not the first time he is sending men on a suicide mission so he can very well read the eyes and the body language of the two boys. Adnan is more nervous than the smooth-skinned but both the boys try to hide their emotions and stay relatively poker-faced.

Uthman feels that he needs to extend his speech in order to instil more courage in the two boys, so he continues, "You two must understand, my brothers, that you are the chosen ones from Allah, the most beneficial and the most merciful. It is a distinction to be extremely proud of. There are many out there who would do anything to get the opportunity to serve directly to the almighty Allah himself. Do you realize what honour this is for you two? This is a guaranteed martyrdom for the cause of Allah. There can be no doubt about your elevation to the highest state in Paradise. I salute you, my heroes, and all the men in the room salute you. Your sacrifice in this world will not be wasted. You will receive the highest recognition in heaven and Allah will forgive all your trespasses and sins. Here, the earth will savour your blood, it will produce more of you and more, until we put an end to these atrocities committed by the Indians on this land of Allah, until our Muslim brothers can breathe freely again under the blue skies of Kashmir. Until every woman and her honour is safe. Until every brother eats freely from his own crop and gives what is left to the less fortunate. My brothers, the world may not know you and may not remember you but I promise that Allah will, his prophets will, his angels will and so does every Muslim who will breathe freely under the sky because of you. We will all thank and remember you, my brothers."

Uthman gets up from his chair and moves across to the other side of the table — coming closer to the boys. The boys stand up, still moved by what he said. It has dawned on them that this is now real and tomorrow they will be sent on a suicide mission. Adnan does not think about the *nihari* and naan bread any more. His brain is running into a panic mode;

all his thoughts are now rooted in fear of death. Death that is now inevitable. There is no turning back, no second chances, this is it. The little child inside Adnan's brain is telling him to do something, maybe try to run away — the child wants to live, play cricket, eat *nihari* — it doesn't want to die. Uthman comes close to the boys and opens his arms wide, expecting the boys to give him a hug. The smooth-skinned steps forward and Adnan shrinks his eyes to control the child in his brain and quickly joins smooth-skinned. They hug.

"May Allah give you two strength and his angels carry you smoothly to heaven." Amaghan then signals Pa Jee to bring in the food. "Once we eat, I will brief you on the mission."

Immediately, food arrives: *nihari, haleem*, grilled chicken tikka, salad, boiled rice and naan breads. The men eat; Adnan tries his best to eat but cannot — how could he? He is going to die tomorrow; will this be his last dinner? Adnan toys with the naan bread and dips it slowly in curry and eats tiny bites. His body language is giving away his nervousness.

Uthman, although fully engrossed in eating the *haleem,* keeps a close eye on Adnan. He is not so much concerned about the smooth-skinned, as he appears excited — it is Adnan who seems to have gone into a shell. "Have some of this *haleem,* Adnan. It is incredibly tasty." Uthman approaches Adnan with affection. "Let's have some, eat like a king — this is your last dinner on this planet and tomorrow you shall be eating with the Prophet himself. Don't you want it?"

"Of course I do — please pass it over to me, Uthman," Adnan responds with a steady voice, concealing his nervousness.

"I'm not talking about the *haleem* any more — you can have it! I meant don't you want it? Martyrdom? And to have dinner with the Prophet Muhammad, peace be upon him?" Uthman smiles and the rest of the men at the table laugh briefly. The food is too good for any of them to pay much attention to what is being said.

"I would love that and I hope that Allah accepts my sacrifice and the Prophet finds me worthy enough to have me in his company," Adnan protests, and comes up with a clever answer.

This time, everyone at the table stops eating and, almost in a perfectly timed chorus, reply, "Amen."

Uthman smiles more in appreciation of the cleverness shown by Adnan rather than feeling confident that Adnan will be able to press the detonation button on the remote that is to blow one and a half tonne of explosives in the back of the truck. He has a plan A up his sleeve that he is not planning to tell the boys. He will only tell them the plan B that will make the boys feel that they are in control. Years of war has taught Uthman that to execute the plan perfectly, he can trust only himself and a close few near him — not every new recruit, no matter how promising they might be. He puts all his focus back to the food that he is genuinely enjoying.

Uthman is a very shrewd operator. His behind-the-scenes team is his most trusted and they are equally loyal to him. Fair play to him, he doesn't play his tricks with them. He treats them as his council and holds very candid consultations with them on every matter: family, finances, recruits, missions, executions and they are not shy in even exchanging pornography with each other on their phones. However, he prefers to treat the recruits hypocritically and with apathy. Outwardly, he treats them like his own children, appears to look after them, but from inside he sees them as sacrificial goats for the cause of Allah. He does not care about their emotions and their wants. In fact, the feeling of fear in the young boys annoys him the most and he immediately begins to dislike them. Hence, the fear he senses in Adnan makes him want to send him on the suicide mission as quickly as possible in order to get rid of him. But he is clever enough and ugly enough to not let his irritation surface in his demeanours and keeps treating Adnan with affection at the dining table.

Uthman finishes his meal and says loudly, "Alhamdulillah!" (Praise be to Allah). He raises his eyebrows and the lines on his forehead are distinctly visible. He looks around the table and everyone else is still eating. He decides to tell the boys the plan. "While you have been here, a couple of our men have put bombs in big concert speakers and put them in the truck. Tomorrow they are celebrating Diwali in the Indian headquarters. It is a festival that they celebrate by lighting lots of candles, setting up fireworks and they dance stupidly to their music. This dark man you see at the table, my angels, is called Shiva, our shining soldier of Allah. Although a Hindu, Shiva has booked himself a place in Jannah by choosing to help the Mujahideen in their cause. The men at the Indian army headquarters have used him as their electrician for a while now and the gates of heaven opened on us when they asked him to arrange the sound system for the Diwali concert tomorrow evening. Allah has gifted us a chance to turn this night into a real festival of lights — real bombs instead of fireworks! The flames from those bombs will be seen right up in the dark sky. The mission is simple. My friend here will accompany you in the truck to the headquarters and introduce you as his helpers, so you should both be getting inside without a problem. Smooth-skinned, you will be driving the truck and Adnan, you will hide behind the speakers. As you know, the truck is fully covered at the back and the doors can be locked both from the inside and the outside. Adnan, you will also wear a suicide jacket tomorrow, not smooth-skin."

"Now listen very carefully, you two," Armghan emphasises, until he has Adnan's complete attention. Adnan has stopped eating whatever little he was eating. Uthman continues with intent in voice and precision in his words. "The gatehouse security should let the truck in after speaking to the Shiva and maybe smooth-skin in the front. Shiva will do the talking only and if, for some reason, they do decide to check the truck by opening its doors then, Adnan, you should stay calm and keep yourself hidden behind the speakers. In that case, Shiva will get out of the truck and accompany the security. But if you sense trouble and feel that you might get caught and will not be able to explain to them that you are sitting in the truck to make sure equipment doesn't fall and you will help the other two in installing it, then press the button of the suicide vest. You'll know how it works — Ustad and Shiva will explain everything to you. But it won't come to that as Allah wills. Once inside the premises, Shiva will guide smooth-skin as to where he should park. He will then come out of the truck alone and make his way to the banquet hall. He will check the situation inside and then signal smooth-skin to come out and then they will open the doors of the back of the truck. Once he asks you, smooth-skinned, to come out and open the back of the truck with him, only then will you come out — otherwise don't under any circumstance. Once the back door of the truck is opened by our friend and smooth-skinned, then, Adnan, you can come out too and help in installing the system. Do as this dark man, Shiva, tells you to do and when you finish the installation smoothly without raising any alarm bells then the three of you will make your way back. We will then detonate the bombs remotely, when the party is in full swing. Do you have any questions?"

Adnan has suddenly found his energy back; he wants to dig into the *nihari* again as this doesn't really sound like a suicide mission any more. Trying to falsely show his disappointment to Uthman, as his desire to impress him hasn't faded one bit, he asks, "This is not a suicide mission and it won't guarantee us martyrdom?"

"Correct! But only if you execute the plan correctly! You will then be heroes instead in the eyes of Allah but not martyrs. I will find another use for you two. Having said that, remember Adnan, if things get out of hand, and only when they get out of hand, then press that button. You will have your martyrdom there and then and so will Smooth-Skinned and Shiva in that case," Uthman instructs.

Everyone smiles and the boys go back to eating. Uthman thinks to himself, 'How naïve the two boys are regards to this. Stupid Adnan thinks that he can fool me by showing his false disappointment for this not to be a suicide mission. I know that how happy and relieved he is from inside. What a coward'! With these thoughts in his head, Uthman then looks at Shiva, the dark Indian man, and who smiles at him with his never-tiring smiling eyes. Uthman smiles back. 'Little do the boys know about the real plan', Uthman thinks to himself.

12

Kashif puts on the blue iPod Nano that he has borrowed from Faisal and plays the Bollywood tunes on high volume. He ventures out of the store, oozing confidence after his meeting with Hayley, goes to Starbucks next door and gets himself a cappuccino with a pack of Belgian waffles. It is a nice crisp autumn morning, so Kashif decides to sit at the coffee table next to the big glass windows with the sun rays falling on his face. He uses his spoon to eat the chocolate-drizzled froth of his cappuccino and reads the book, *The Alchemist*. He feels that he has just fitted right in the city and the air of this fast-paced city of London has already started to work to erase the difficult memories of the past. He decides to skip visiting King's College but instead to walk all the way up to St. Paul's Cathedral. He has seen St. Paul's Cathedral on the internet and remembers that Princess Diana and Prince Charles chose to get married there. He has worked out, looking at the map Hayley printed out for him, that the cathedral is a straight walk up the New Gate Street from where he sat in Starbucks on Chancery Lane. Breathing the fresh London air, compared to Karachi, and looking at nicely dressed people walking past him, Kashif feels a deep sense of liberation and joy inside him. He arrives at St. Paul's Cathedral in almost no time and feels a burst of energy inside him. He enters the magnificent building to the practice of the cathedral choir playing Bach's Cello Suite no.

1; he is completely awestruck by the magic of the moment. The beautiful cathedral, along with the amazing music being played simultaneously, is something that he has never experienced before. He stands still just inside the entrance and allows the beauty of the moment to sink in; he feels that energy of this moment is making all his sorrows go away. He remains in the trance-like state, forgiving his father's killer, forgiving himself and forgiving his God! He cannot still rationalise that God had to take away his father when he was still so young and had so much to offer. Instead, he tells himself that not all things are meant to be understood and that he should live in the moment. And this moment is full of love and peace that he should fully embrace. He takes a few steps forward and decides to sit at the edge of the last bench and silences himself completely. Without realizing, he has spent just about an hour in this blissful place, while the choir have played different tunes and are now singing Bach's *St. Matthew's Passion — Wir setzen uns mit Tränen nieder*. The music runs through his veins now and he decides to walk back to the store after this piece finishes as he wants to leave on a high.

With his soul being refreshed by the experience, Kashif blissfully comes back to the store half an hour early. Haley looks at him and says, "You really want this job, mate! Don't you?"

Kashif hurriedly replies, "Yes! Of course!"

Hayley smiles back and tells him to wait for her in the pub opposite to the store. She hands him a ten-pound note, asking him to get whatever he wants and to get a glass of house white wine for her. She tells him that she will see him there in about ten minutes. Kashif gives her the money back and says that he would like to do the honours. He orders himself a glass of house red and a glass of Pinot Grigio for Haley. He then makes himself comfortable on the sofa next to the window while Bach's Cello Suite no.1 still playing in his mind. He doesn't wait for Hayley and instead starts sipping his wine. Hayley doesn't waste much time either and quickly touches up her make-up and puts on her jacket; she already fancies him. There is something refreshing about him, she thinks to herself. She joins Kashif within five minutes of him leaving the store.

"Thank you, Kashif! You are a real gentleman. First, let's get the important stuff out of the way; you have the job, so congratulations! I have asked the supervisor to do your paperwork. Once we finish from here, you can go back to the store. He is there till close tonight so don't worry about the time; you have plenty! Unless you need to be somewhere else?"

Kashif smiles and replies, "No! Not at all! Thank you, Hayley! You are ever so kind! And incredibly beautiful! I'm lucky to have you as my first manager in the UK."

Hayley smiles back and asks Kashif to bring his drink along to the back garden of the pub so that she could have a smoke. They go outside and sit next to each other; she lights her Marlboro and offers one to Kashif, which he accepts. She then lifts glass up and says, "Cheers to your new job!" They both touch their glasses together.

Hayley downs a good amount of wine in the first go and looks at Kashif. He is still in a trance-like feeling from the visit to the cathedral and with the red wine in the system, he appears to be very content.

Hayley cleverly asks him, "Tell me, Kashif — what are you thinking?"

Kashif looks at her with irresistible intensity and, with a smile through his eyes, responds in a very calming voice, "Please don't think I'm weird but I'll tell you honestly what I'm thinking; I'm imagining how, in ancient times, men work tirelessly in the fields during the morning. Then in the evening they come home and rest while the women cook for them; they wash themselves together and then eat dinner. Then they go out, have a drink near the cool fountain and kiss. Then they come home and make love endlessly. Sometimes they invite prostitutes that can be either a woman or a man, depending on what the couple agree. They go some evenings to the theatre; men and women would sit shoulder to shoulder to each other and enjoy the performances by different artists. These artists stay mostly single but are never short of making love amongst each other. The couples watching would sip wine and eat grapes, berries and nuts while enjoying the show. During the day, women have different tasks: from going to the market in order to shop for food and clothes to teaching children or nurse the sick. They are free to choose any profession that they prefer. If the man earns enough, maybe by working in an important bureaucratic post, the couple can afford to keep a servant. Young female maids are not allowed when the couples themselves are young, so the house helpers are mostly older women or older men. Life continues in endless hard work, but also with intense love for each other."

Kashif leans forwards towards Hayley and kisses her. Hayley, captivated by the intensity of Kashif's eyes and his words, although not understanding mostly what he has said, kisses him back.

13

"I have never had sex with a girl before — you are my first."

Kashif speaks softly while looking at Hayley's bedroom ceiling as they both lie naked next to each other under the duvet. Hayley comes closer and kisses Kashif on his ears. There is a sudden silence broken only by slow and constant breathing of both Hayley and Kashif. Hayley then holds his hand and gently puts it down on top of her naval. Kashif realizes that from there onwards his hand has a mind of its own. He drags it slowly keeping it firm against Hayley's skin, applying gentle pressure. Hayley closes her eyes and surrenders herself in the moment. She keeps her hand tenderly on Kashif's hand but does not try to guide it. Kashif is extremely slow with his movements. He reads every movement that Hayley makes as his hand ventures further down her body. His fingers gently forcing their way through her soft pubic hair while he still applies pressure on her groin with the base of his palm. Hayley's breathing turns heavy. The sound of her breath, the feel of her soft skin and the excitement of the moment is pushing Kashif's penis hard against the duvet. Soon Kashif finds his fingers reaching the soft and wet lips of Hayley's vagina. Applying the same pressure, he finds his index finger slip inside Hayley. Every movement made by the couple feels natural. He hears a little cry of pain and pleasure originating from deep inside Hayley, and somehow making it out through her mouth. Her body moves like a wave, up and down towards the ceiling and then pushes back deep into the foam of the bed. Moving his finger gently inside her, Kashif uses his other hand to fondle her breasts. He does so carefully and keeps both his hands occupied in order to give Hayley continuous pleasure. He then looks at Hayley's face and finds her completely lost in the moment. Seeing her in such a blissful state, Kashif himself is overcome by a feeling of freedom and serenity. Hayley's features enhance this blissful state; Kashif has never seen a woman look so beautiful. There is no feeling of rush of blood or nervousness in Kashif's veins and he thinks to himself, without uttering any words. 'This is heaven'!

Kashif lifts himself up, turns over on top of Hayley — she looks at him in the eyes with immense intensity, and whispers to him, "I want you."

Kashif then slowly pushes down on her; his penis feels her wet vagina. Hayley then opens her legs slightly wider. With one gentle thrust, Kashif finds himself inside her. Hayley cries louder this time — her tone is more of pleasure than pain.

14

"Here you go, Shiva. A hundred thousand Indian rupees in cash — count them if you like, count them if you like. I don't want any hiccups tomorrow; make sure everything goes according to plan." Uthman hands over a black Nike gym bag to Shiva, full of thousand-rupee notes.

"Like I said, I have already spoken to Captain Naek a few times. Just last night I spoke with him again when I arranged for him to come to the brothel to shag Pinky, his favourite teenager. You know very well that I'm more than just an electrician to them: in fact, firstly I'm a pimp, then only a handy man! I thanked him for giving me the tender to install the sound system so I can earn a few extra bucks. Anyway, Captain Naek said that he has personally authorised for the truck to be let in and has reserved a place in the parking lot inside the headquarters which a distance away from the banquet hall. He also said that I should come and see him and he will escort me and the boys to the banquet hall to set up the sound system. He has also arranged for us to have free lunch from the mess canteen. What a generous man! Now, once I put the speakers in the hall, I'll excuse the boys, saying that I need to go and see the Captain to tell him that our work is done and he can come and have a look. I'll also make sure that the boys understand that under no circumstances they are to leave the banquet hall until I instruct them to. Then, instead of going back to the Captain Naek, I'll head back to the truck and drive out. I'll tell the security that I have forgotten a few bits that I'll need for the installation and will be back with them. No one will suspect me, trust me, as I've been in and out a few times. Once I'm at a fair distance outside and still receiving signals, I'll press the button to detonate the bombs. And BOOM! I'll abandon the truck in the woods and pick the car you've left there for me, then start my journey all the way down to Karachi with my new identity under the protection of Pakistan army. And then later, at some point, move back to India. Execute this perfectly and then I'm never to be seen in this neck of the woods ever again. Simple!" Shiva calmly replies, with his signature smile, already contemplating his new life in Goa, where he plans to open a little bar for the tourists.

"OK, it sounds good but just make sure you don't fuck up anything, Shiva. Neither you nor the boys should get caught, any under circumstances, before the explosion. Also, I don't want them to discover the tunnel. We may still need to use it in the future. You have to get this right, Shiva. I mean, if the boys get caught or if the army figure out what is inside the speakers, then that will be the end of the road for this plan. Remember, the boys will always be thinking that they need a cue from you when to blow up their suicide vests as well, so keep reassuring them that you know what you are doing and the time to blow up their vests will come soon. If anything goes tit-faced then we, 'The Army of Muhammad', will have no choice but to ambush the headquarters and you know what that means; to each his own." Uthman squeezed his beard twice with his right hand as if somehow to convey the gravity of his words to Shiva.

"I know, Uthman — trust me it will not come to that. I have spent time gaining the trust of these men from the headquarters. I provide them with the sweetest commodities their little money can buy; alcohol, drugs and prostitutes! I know what most of them like; the captain himself likes to be punched in the balls by Pinky. Just hard enough that he feels the pain but doesn't break his ball! It is a very weird way to get turned on; that is what Pinky tells me. So, these men let me roam freely inside the headquarters, like I pose no threat. Anyway, don't put the suicide vest or a gun on any of the boys like we talked about. I know you have told Adnan earlier that he is to wear one. The army might do a security search on them and then we will be screwed."

"I don't need a pimp to remind me of my tasks. You have your money, Shiva — make sure you do your bit properly and don't worry about the boys; Ustad will take care of them. They will not cause you any problems, you have my word. Adnan will wear a suicide jacket and he won't get searched. You make sure of that. Now, I wish you well for tomorrow and for your future life as a pimp in some other place! Remember — do not try to contact me, or any one of my brothers, ever. May Allah be with you!"

"But I have one question for you, Uthman. Why not wait till the party starts and detonate remotely yourself? You will kill more people surely, wouldn't you?" Shiva enquires with a baffled look on his face.

Uthman replies in disgust, "You are a lowly Hindu, aren't you? How can I expect you to know the basic etiquette of war! No women and children. Allah doesn't want us Muslims to kill children, women, elderly or disabled. Only men and traitors like yourself! And trust me, there will be plenty during the day. And I want them to believe that it was a suicide mission carried out by two boys working for 'The Army of Muhammad'. As after the detonation, we will claim responsibility. Anyway, we can't keep the boys till the party starts — what excuse they will have to stay this long? To check the women out? Now, let this be the last time we see each other or speak; never again, Shiva, never ever again!"

15

Layla invariably keeps talking to Siddiq about her husband, Omar, whenever he comes to teach her daughter and sometimes just even name dropping. Telling him little stories about her husband feels mostly out of place in their conversation. It is as if she does it to remind herself that she is married to Omar and that she shouldn't be leading on this young and handsome boy, Siddiq, who is only a tutor for her daughter. She knows that, in her hearts of hearts, she wants to press Siddiq's young and strong body against hers. Even though she is concerned about her husband's increasing interest in Madiha, Layla has no intentions of cheating on him.

Siddiq has sensed that Layla is into him. It is easy for him to sense this; each afternoon when he finishes tutoring her daughter, she brings him tea with something to eat. She sits down with him every time, dresses neatly and carries a conversation. Siddiq has also worked out that Layla is not completely content with her marital life at the moment. She complains to Siddiq about her boredom when her husband is away and she has no life other than looking after her clingy kids.

This routine carries on for some time until one afternoon, Layla comes up to Siddiq when he is finished teaching her daughter. She sends her daughter back to her room, sits right next to Siddiq on the couch and says, "I have got you some green tea, Siddiq, but sorry, I couldn't prepare anything for you to snack on today. I had a weird dream while I was taking my afternoon nap. I have been thinking about it since. I saw that a war has broken out between India and Pakistan. It is chaos everywhere and the Pakistani government has asked for every healthy man over the age of sixteen to join the armed forces. Omar, being a dumb enthusiastic patriot, has decided to leave us three and his parents behind and join the army, even though it isn't mandatory for any citizen to join. So, I beg him not to go but, as always, he doesn't listen to me. He packs two full suitcases as if he is leaving us for good and, with a determined face, walks out of the door.

"Things turn from bad to worse for us; we are losing badly. The Americans have joined the war in support of the Indians. The Chinese support us but not to the same extent as the US support the Indians, and the Russians are silent. Then a bomb gets dropped near my house during the night. A little block of shops a mile down the road is completely destroyed; there have been a few casualties but everyone that I know is safe. But I don't know where Omar is; I haven't heard from him and that makes me worried sick. Nevertheless, you come here every week day to teach my daughter and this familiar routine gives me peace. You chose not to join the army; you said you are too clever to take orders from someone else and not stupid to volunteer yourself for the war. You cannot take pleasure in taking a life even though they have come to take yours. You say that you would rather be killed and rather be oppressed than be an oppressor. I like that about you.

"Are you this clever, Siddiq, in real life? Or is it just my perception of you?"

Layla's hair is loosely tied and she has put very low-tone make-up on with a red lipstick that makes her voluptuous lips even more prominent. She had taken a bath earlier, with white tea essence bath foam, and smells lovely. She is not wearing any panties under her light-blue shalwar kameez[1], printed with white flowers. Her loosely-held white dupatta[2] slides down from her shoulders onto her lap as she leans towards Siddiq while asking him this question. Her cleavage is now exposed and she places her right hand on Siddiq's thigh. Before he could answer her rhetorical question, Layla kisses him. Caught by surprise, Siddiq kisses her back forcefully.

"Gentle — use your lips only, not your teeth."

With their lips locked together, Layla guides the novice and excited Siddiq through his first kiss. Siddiq heeds her direction and manoeuvres his lips softly — too softly — overcompensating for the earlier anxiousness. But the excitement in his body is being felt elsewhere. He has such a massive erection that he feels the need to open the zip of his jeans and let the monster out, or else it will break itself against the denim fabric. He holds Layla's left breast tightly, squeezing it and then starting from below her ribs, he presses upwards onto her right breast with his other hand. Feeling a tingling in her vagina, Layla pulls his right hand off her breasts and puts it on her groin area.

Her vagina is warm, soft and very wet. As if Siddiq's hand is programmed to deliver pleasure, his fingers start to make their way through her very soft and tiny pubic hair onto the lips of her vagina. Layla crams his hand tightly between her thighs, overcoming by the sweet sensation. Siddiq has gained in confidence; he kisses her more passionately and rubs his thumb on her nipple, which is fully erect. He tries to open up his palm against her thighs and manages to put his index finger inside Layla's wet and warm vagina. She sighs and tilts her head backwards and their lips unlock. Siddiq sneaks a look. With her eyes closed and her neck fully stretched and her jugular vein pressing hard against her skin, Siddiq moves forwards and starts kissing her on the neck. He goes hard, like a vampire, but it has a reverse effect. Instead of going deeper into pleasure, Layla becomes more alert. She doesn't want to have a hickey so that Omar finds out what she has been up to. She gently pushes Siddiq back and kisses him on his lips again.

She then takes her hand down his groin area and finds it, rubbing strongly against a massive erection that has overtaken Siddiq. She holds back from the kisses and rushes to unzip his pants and drags his penis out through the opening in his underwear. Siddiq's penis is circumcised, has more girth then length and the head is dark purple — a healthy-looking penis. She starts jerking him off and returns back to kiss him again. For less than half a minute, they both have their hands massaging each other's private parts with their eyes closed as they continue to kiss until, all of a sudden, Siddiq rolls back on his chair, looks at heaven, and with a single grunt, ejaculates profusely. Layla could feel his warm cum falling on her hand and she continues to jerk him off until there is no more sperm coming out. His penis still pulsating though.

Then, with absolutely no emotions, almost in a robotic manner, she instructs Siddiq to clean himself and gives him the tissue box. Siddiq wipes out the wet cum and Layla takes the tissues off him. She then disappears into her room via dropping the waste in the kitchen bin. Her daughter is playing a car racing game on the Xbox in Layla's room. Siddiq uses the toilet and waits in the study for Layla to come back, but she doesn't. Confused what to do, Siddiq waits for another ten minutes and then decides to leave the house.

Sat on the bed watching her daughter play, guilt starts to creep into Layla's head. 'Why did I do it? Why did I cheat on Omar? Was it even cheating? We didn't have sex! In fact, I didn't even enjoy it. If it was any good, probably I would've felt better as now I feel guilty for doing something that wasn't even fun!'

She immediately gets out of her bed and runs a shower. Feeling clean, she decides to pray. "Allah, forgive me for my trespass. It was a mistake, I shouldn't have done it, please forgive me and keep my marriage safe. Safe from any harm and especially from that bitch, Madiha! Please don't let her steal my husband."

She greets Omar warmly when he comes back to the house and gives her all the signs that she is horny tonight. At bed time, she turns off the lights quickly and gets fifty seconds of pleasure from Omar.

A couple of days later, after she feels the dust has settled, she wraps a hundred percent tip for Siddiq with the existing month's salary and hands it over to him, thanking him for the hard work he has put in for her daughter but now it is time that she feels that she can get back into the same routine of teaching her daughter herself. Siddiq politely receives the envelope and says thank you. He finishes teaching her daughter for the day, wishes her goodbye and best of luck and walks out with his head down.

Siddiq heads straight to Abu Bakr mosque avoiding contact with anyone. The mosque is relatively quiet as it is not yet the prayer time. He goes deep into prayer in hope of forgiveness from Allah and a brighter future for himself and his family. After finishing his prayers, Siddiq whispers believing that Allah is listening to him,

"O'Allah! Please forgive me as I have sinned. I was weak and succumbed to my carnal desires. I promise that I will not touch a woman again other than whoever you choose for me to marry. O'Allah you are the biggest forgiver; please I beg you to pardon me at this instance and I will not repeat my mistake. O'Allah please bestow your blessing on me and on my family. Please grant me a life where I have good health, a good job, an obedient wife and beautiful children. And please give me the chance to look after my parents when they are old and cannot look after themselves. Lastly, please grant us all Muslims a place in Jannah including Layla and forgive her too. That is all I want from life... Amen"

16

"So, are you a Muslim?"

Hayley passes the clear blue lighter to Kashif after lighting up her Marlboro cigarette. With her hair loose, hanging down to her shoulders, wearing Kashif's grey King's College London's hoodie and her black panties, she looks ruggedly sexy. Perhaps she knows herself that she looks very attractive. She has a confident and naughty smile on her face while she asks the question as if to suggest to Kashif that even if he is a Muslim, he cannot be good one. Muslims aren't allowed to have sex before marriage or a similar bond between man and woman. Hayley's blue eyes shine so promisingly that Kashif changes his mind before lighting his cigarette and kisses her passionately. He then puts his arms around and over the top of Hayley's shoulders. He looks carefully and quickly around the backyard where they stood, making sure that no one else is listening. Kashif behaves as if he has a big secret to share with Hayley. The evening wind blows strongly; Hayley takes a sudden puff to keep her cigarette lit, fearing the wind would turn it off. Kashif tries to hide the slight guilt he feels about what he is going to say to Hayley as he does not want to lie to her, so he replies light heartedly, "I don't know, Hayley — not according to the classic definition at least! I drink, I eat pork and I just lost my virginity with the ugliest girl in the world!"

They both smile at each other, Kashif decides to talk more about it. He wants to know the answer to this question for himself more so then Hayley. After the death of his father, he has been thinking differently about religion; things have changed. He felt a deep anger towards religion when he was grieving for his father's demise. He blamed religion and thought it was the only culprit behind his father's death. Now, much calmer, he wants to get in touch with his inner beliefs, so he continues, "I have my reservations on religion, Hayley. Religion is meant to break boundaries between people but instead it creates more boundaries amongst us. To me, it does more harm than good. People kill under its name and what is worse is that they feel perfectly OK doing so! In fact, they get motivated by the rewards it promises to give them in return for their inhuman deeds.

"I think I still believe in God though, but he might not necessarily be called Allah as they refer to him. I see God as more of a creator who loves its creation, his animals, his nature, his universe, and doesn't interfere with the daily activities between its creations. I think he designed the universe in such a way that things take care of themselves; everything balances out one way or the other — some quickly and some not so — may be sort of like karma, if you want to call it that. So no, my beliefs now don't make me a Muslim any more; an agnostic maybe, if I'm honest!

"Sometimes I have so many questions in my head that I just give up trying to find answers in religion or even try to rationalize them in any other way. So now, I don't know about what is the right or the wrong thing to do according to Islam. I just follow my heart and say to myself to let God be my judge;

fuck religion and its followers. If there is a God and I get to meet him, then I'll ask him all the questions in my head and he'll answer me if he so wishes and maybe he will also tell me whether I was right in following my heart or whether I should have followed his Quran. He will be then be my judge, and that will be the end of it. If hell exists, like they say, and if God puts me there, then I am happy to burn but I won't burn myself here on earth and then get burnt again! You know what I mean? Simply, I want to live! In fact, tell you what Hayley — I know I won't burn anywhere; I'll be ok wherever I will be."

Hayley listens intently, and then tells Kashif, "God loves you, Kashif — I'm quite sure of that! And by simply following your heart I cannot see you being in the wrong here. I believe that it must take a lot of courage to think differently — in fact, being so honest in your thinking, despite growing up in a society which seems pretty strict, at least from what I see from the news. But I have a question. I mean, it's probably a silly question and you might not know the answer. Anyway, I was curious as to why Muslim women cover themselves — like their hair and face?"

Kashif finally lights up his Marlboro Red, exhales the smoke in a manner that he took a sigh, and replies, "I think I know the answer to this, Hayley. Back in the old days, the Arabs were barbaric in their ways of life; raping women at will and burying their daughters alive in the ground simply because they were embarrassed to have them. To give birth to a daughter was considered as some sort of a weakness — I don't know. Anyway, women were instructed or asked by Allah to cover themselves properly and not to wear anything revealing in public so as not to get teased, assaulted or raped by the mostly immoral and uneducated Arab men. This was basically for their safety and protection. Now, in the context, I sort of understand that. I mean, still in these times a girl would try to avoid walking down a dark alley wearing a miniskirt with hungry men lurking around, shouting catcalls or abuse. She'd probably alter her route or maybe cover her cleavage with a scarf or try and pull down her skirt a little bit; sort of a natural behaviour to avoid any unwanted attention or trouble from any scumbags. Again, back then, Arabia was going through a period of transition; work was being carried out by the Prophet and his disciples to educate the Arabs, teaching them basic morals and way of life. So Allah's request to women to cover themselves during this time was stemmed more in caution for their own sake until the Prophet developed the Arabic mentality to a humane level; basically, until the men have some fucking morals! The main point here was for the women to not draw unwanted attention towards them by the crass Arabs, so that they don't get teased and so on.

"Keeping this point in mind, nowadays when a woman drapes herself in a black hijab from head to toe and jumps on a London underground, wouldn't she draw unwanted attention towards herself? People might think that she is a suicide bomber! I wouldn't be totally surprised if she is teased or even racially abused by some idiots. So when they live here in Europe, in these modern times, they should dress normally like women dress here — jeans, t-shirt, whatever, and avoid being singled out.

"If I take you to Saudi Arabia with me, Hayley, then, knowing you, you would also put a scarf around your head to show respect to their culture and also avoid raising any eye brows. I know that because you are humble enough to respect other cultures and try to fit in. So I don't know why the Muslim women feel the need to cover themselves in a place like Europe, where doing so may cause them more problems, if anything, and like I just explained to you, their Allah doesn't really want them to do that either. The Muslims here have lost the plot! I'm sorry it's a very long answer to your rather simple question." Kashif takes another puff of his cigarette.

Hayley replies quickly with a smile, "Ah! But rather a good answer! Damn, boy, you are in a mood tonight! I feel like asking you a few more questions now!"

"Go on then, my lady, fire away!" Kashif feels happy because Hayley seems to agree with his interpretations of the rules of Islam.

"OK, so what's with Muslims not eating pork? Haram and all that."

"I don't know about Muslims but I eat it! You know I loved the spicy sausage that I tried the other day at Zizzi's! What was it called? N'duja, I believe," Kashif replies candidly, but Hayley gives him an unimpressed look. Kashif then goes deeper in thinking. "I honestly don't know but some things are just carried over from the Jews and their Torah to the Quran. Apparently, one of the sages from Jews has some issue with the pigs and possibly with the dogs — it was to do with their claws being split or something. Anyway, God ordered the Jews not to raise or eat pork. Now, whether it was God who ordered that or the sage himself depends on what one wants to believe. Then the Quran, I guess, followed suit and banned eating the flesh of the swine.

I think both the Jews and Muslims are more or less disgusted with the poor little pig. To be fair, science is also not a big fan of pork either, but then I guess all kinds of red processed meat isn't really healthy for us anyway!

"Then there is also this thing about dogs with the Muslims that I don't get. I had a dog once as a child and I remember my grandma emotionally blackmailed my mom to get rid of it. She told my mother that she won't be allowed to visit her grave if she doesn't get rid of the cute little poodle. A bit harsh on my mom as I wanted the dog but she had to give it away to one of her Christian friends. I'm all up for not eating dogs, obviously, but there is a thing about Muslims keeping the dogs in the house. They say the dogs bark at the angels and drive them out of the house! I mean, how ridiculous! I think the poor things bark when they are scared, upset, want food, have seen a ghost or simply staring at a branch of tree that moves suddenly! But not angels, for God's sake! But who cares about what I think, ey? There is actually a verse in the Quran called 'Al Kahf', where two wise men and their dog were protected by Allah from a tyrant king or some bad people — I don't exactly know. Anyway, they hid themselves in a cave, with their dog sat at the entrance guarding it.

"Now Allah put the wise men to sleep for three hundred years and kept their dog on the watch, for the same period of time; don't ask me how though! Anyway, when these wise men woke up, they found their dog exactly at the same place alive and well. Probably asking for food as soon as they woke up! The men didn't realize that they had slept for such a long period of time, but when they came out from their cave with their dog, the whole scenery outside had changed. The world had developed, the society become educated and people, friendly. The men, with their dog, ventured into the market; one of them took one of his coins out to get some food. The vendor looked at them with amazement and asked them where they got this precious antique? The vendor was a good man and helped the wise men to sell these coins at a handsome price, as such that they lived happily ever after — with their dog, of course!

Now, you tell me, sweetheart, how does a poor dog get to be a bad one in this story? It is the Quran talking good things about a dog, not me. So, I think there might be another sage or maybe a caliph in the case of Muslims who, for some reason, did not like dogs and banned Muslims from having them as their pets. Poor little dogs — majority of them end up as strays in Pakistan, living off rubbish and some rough kids throwing stones at them!" Kashif looks at Hayley, visibly angered by the way his people and other Muslims think about certain concepts.

Hayley finds this look of Kashif incredibly attractive. "My intelligent hottie! Come here, my sage!"

She holds Kashif's face in her hands gently; they both kiss passionately.

17

"I cannot tell you, Smooth Skin, how I am feeling tonight. It feels that the world is moving around me and I am standing away watching it from a distance — just looking at people go about their daily business. Some of them are taking a moment to look around the beautiful hills surrounding the valley before returning to their businesses or homes, their families, their wives and their children. I have come so far away from my family; I wish I could speak to them one more time before tomorrow. Before I die, I want my mother's voice to comfort me. If you survive this, Smooth Skin, and I don't, then please do me a little favour and tell my mother that I love her!"
Adnan speaks strongly but Smooth Skin listens to him with some disinterest. "We are not going to die tomorrow, Adnan," replies Smooth Skin, while still concentrating on the game that he is playing on his mobile. "You remember what Uthman told us, don't you?" he said, implying that Adnan should remember the mission briefing by Uthman. "We will simply install the speakers containing the bombs and then come out of there safely without doing anything suspicious. Then Uthman will detonate the bombs when we are back at the base. Following that, we will all go to hiding in Pakistan — maybe all the way down to Karachi. You will then be re-united with your family! The suicide vests are just a precaution if things get out of hand; but, trust me, they won't. So relax now, my friend!"

For a little while, Adnan ponders over Smooth Skin's response but then continues, "I don't know, Smooth Skin, I have a feeling that I will die tomorrow and that makes me scared. I cannot think properly; everything appears hazy to me. I cannot make any relation with my surroundings any more. I genuinely don't know what is going on here. I am so confused!"

Smooth Skin puts away his mobile phone this time and responds with a serious face. "Look, Adnan, remember fear can kill you faster than a bullet. Now calm the fuck down and stop being a pussy. Allah is with us and all will be fine as long as you have faith in him. More than ever we need to have our wits with us tomorrow, otherwise we will actually need to use those bloody suicide vests! Think about it my friend; in fact, think about those sexy virgins! Which one would you fuck first — the blonde ones with blue eyes or a hot black or a sexy sultry Arabic one, ey?! I'm definitely going to go for a black panther! That's my dream... Come on, friend, cheer up! You will finally get to have sex!"

Smooth Skin laughs and Adnan smiles back in return. "Don't forget, we can have seventy-two of them, Smooth Skin! I will make combinations of each and every kind. Tell you what — I'll make one with a big thick penis and give it to you as a gift! Anyway, you might want to think of having sex with all those virgins but right now I can't even pee let alone get an erection! You don't get it, Smooth Skin! I don't know if you even have a family!" Adnan slips back into his worrying state of mind.

Smooth Skin does not reply to Adnan, but instead wished him goodnight and tries to fall asleep. Adnan couldn't sleep all night and hearing Smooth Skin snore next to him did not help either. 'He must be at the prime of his faith to sleep like a baby on the night before he is meant to die the following day! Either that or he is too stupid and actually believes that we will all come out alive and that the Indian army won't come chasing after us and kill us! I've heard someone say once that ignorance provides the happiest life; it seems to be true in Smooth Skin's case'. Uthman thinks this to himself.

Early in the morning, around half past five, both the boys are out of their beds to offer the morning prayers. Adnan knows the Quran by heart so he leads the prayers with Smooth Skin praying behind him. Adnan prays sincerely, asking Allah for courage to carry out the mission without being caught and that he comes out alive. He begs Allah to ensure his safety and that he would return to live with his family and parents after the mission is complete. Emotions taking him over and with tears in his eyes, he continues to beg Allah for his life and admits to his fears that he is not ready to die yet for any cause.

Around ten a.m., when both the boys are taking a nap and Adnan finally gets to sleep a little, there is a knock on the door. It's Ustad. He carries a big gym bag with him, stuffed with two suicide vests for the boys. The vest is made out of jute and is sturdy. It has eight large pockets, four in front and four at the back. Seven of the eight pockets are filled with explosives while the top right pocket has a wireless radio receiver hidden inside the explosives.

He also brings the boys breakfast; tea with milk and aloo paratha, which is a wheat-based naan bread with potato filling. They have breakfast together; not a word is being said between the three of them. Adnan has lost his appetite; he slowly drinks his tea, looking into the empty spaces, and takes only a couple of bites of aloo paratha. The food is cold but that doesn't bother Smooth Skin — he eats like a hungry man with no worries.

After they had finished breakfast, they gather in the toilet. Ustad asks the boys to take off their shirt. He then pulls out the suicide vest and puts it around Adnan first. It feels heavy. Adnan lowers his eyes and has a good long look at the explosives but doesn't say a word. He then asks him to wear an extra-large size blue hoodie that he has brought with him. The hoodie reads 'Nike' in white colour and has a big tick symbol on it; ironically, on the back it reads 'Just do it'. Branded but slightly defective clothes are easy and cheap to find in both India and Pakistan, as many of them are manufactured locally and the waste gets sold in the local market. He then asks Adnan to wear his jeans and get ready. He then turns to Smooth Skin and performs the same act as he did on Adnan, only this time he has a different hoodie for Smooth Skin. It is black in colour and simply says 'FILA' in white where the left pocket would be on a normal shirt.

Both the boys are ready, with suicide vests installed, up and running on their bodies! Ustad then kisses the boys' foreheads and tells them that in case of real emergency, all they need to do is hold the small white button on their vest for about five seconds and the vest will blow up. However, as per Uthman's instructions, the button is disabled and won't work if the boys press them. The bomb can only go off with the remotes that Uthman and Shiva each have.

"May the Allah and his angels guide you to success, my heroes!" With a smile on his face, Ustad leaves the boys.

Just after midday, Shiva comes to them with the truck containing tonnes of explosives packed inside the big JVC speakers. Shiva has a remote for it but so does Uthman, and only Ustad and Uthman know that.

"Hello boys! How are we feeling today?" Shiva greets the boys with chirpiness that the boys find surprising. He doesn't seem to be at all flustered by the occasion. Instead, he seems unusually excited, as if he is looking forward to it!

He lifts their hoodies and checks their suicide vests. With no expression on his face, he pulls them back down. He then asks both the boys to get into the back of the truck and starts to drive.

18

Indian Television Breaking News — Feb 2001 14:38

"Early reports from Indian army headquarters in Srinagar — there has been a suicide attack at the premises with six confirmed dead including two suicide bombers and four Indian army officials. The number of casualties, are likely to rise as many are reported to be seriously injured in what appears to be a terrorist attack. It is believed that apart from the two suicide vests found, other more powerful bombs were also installed in the speakers that were put in the GHQ mess hall, to play music during the celebration of the Diwali festivities this evening. Police and the army are hunting for a suspect who seems to be at large and goes by the name of Shiva Kumar. It is believed that the suspect is driving a white truck; the police have issued this sketch of the man who is believed to be in his late thirties and fluent in Hindi, Punjabi and English. If you have seen the man or know of his whereabouts then please get in touch with your local authorities. There is a reward of RS. 150,000 that the Indian army has offered to anyone providing information about the suspect leading to his capture.

"The chief of Indian army, Staff General Rahul Sharma, has blamed the Pakistani terror group Jaish-e Muhammad for the attack and has condemned the Pakistani government in shamelessly supporting the terror group. The Pakistani government and its army are yet to respond to these allegations."

"Allah hu Akbar!" Armaghan and his comrades hug each other with joy after witnessing the news. Their mission is a resounding success.

"So you did put the suicide vests on the boys then? Because the explosion seems massive!" Pa Jee asks Uthman, with a mischievous smile in his eyes.

Uthman smiles back while nodding his head in agreement. "They were going to die inside the headquarters anyway; by putting extra bombs on their bodies I was able to increase the impact of the explosion. My men tell me the whole place is gone down in rubble. There are at least twenty to thirty motherfucking Indian soldiers dead. Plus, there is a huge loss to their equipment, their army mobile machine gun carriers, their cars and I've heard that even one of the tanks went upside down due to the intensity of the explosion! Obviously, the Indian national TV news and media would never admit to the extent of the damage, as it will show that we really hurt them!"

"So what's next?" Pa Jee now looks intently at Uthman, realising that he is cunning beyond his anticipation of him.

"Our job is done for now, until we wait for the next mission sent down to us by Chief Osama Bin Laden himself! Yes, Pa Jee, don't be surprised! I was guaranteed a senior place in Osama's Taliban if I were to carry out this mission successfully. I can imagine the day when I will get to kiss Osama's hands and meet the true caliph of Muslims myself. As far as the politics go, the Indian government will blame Pakistan and Pakistan will blame other agencies or even Indian nationalist parties — that they have carried out this attack to increase tension between India and Pakistan. Same old, same old — these two countries will always argue and fight but I don't think that there will be another war between them like in 1965 and 1971. There are too many external political factors involved; Russia, China and US have their own interests in the region. All of this will dilute, so, for now, we just wait and see."

"What if they come to my place asking questions about Shiva and about the boys?" Pa Jee asks Uthman, with a slightly concerned look on his face.

"The two boys are blown into bits. They were here for such a short time only; no one recognises them. As far as Shiva goes, they know that he knew every restaurant, pub, brothel and their owners. So you will say to them what everyone else will say and that he was a customer of the restaurant like everyone else. If anyone needs to be worried then it should be the brothel owner as Shiva has fucked off in the white truck that he borrowed from him for a day!" Uthman replies calmly, as he has covered every aspect and believes that everything will be fine.

"I'm just not comfortable that they have put such a big reward for Shiva's head and if they found the identity of the boys and begin asking any of my customers then someone might say something. A few of my customers must have seen the boys walk in my restaurant the other night, surely?" Pa Jee continues to challenge Uthman's logic, mainly for his own piece of mind.

"Look, Pa Jee" Uthman continues in a stern tone

"If you need to escape to Pakistan under a separate identity, all you need to do is to tell me and I'll arrange everything for you. You know that very well. So don't worry — everything will be fine. If the questioning gets out of hand than we will do something about it. Regarding your customers, we have done the research. Ustad and I know every fat fucker that was eating in your restaurant the other night! They haven't got a clue who was coming in and going out as they were too busy filling up their ugly bellies! Besides, like I said, the guys did not stay in the restaurant for long, did not serve any customers — just said hello to you and went inside. Also, the Indian army would not be able to picture them as they are blown into fragments! I connected their suicide vests with the bombs in the speakers so as soon as Shiva pressed the button both the boys and the speakers detonated at the same time! No way will they be recognisable! Did you see their faces or sketches on the news like Shiva's? No, right! Lastly, we changed the plan last minute. Shiva drove the truck himself inside the headquarters with both the boys in the back of the truck. I made that call because then no Indian soldier would've seen the boys to give some kind of evidence to be able to picture the suspects. I told Shiva if he does get asked by the gate keeper, he need not to hide the fact that the boys are in the back of the truck. Instead, he can tell them that the boys are there holding the expensive speakers and the audio system together to avoid damage in transit."

"One last question, Uthman, then I promise that I will shut up. All of this is a clever plan, but how did Shiva agree to put the boys in the back as, if something would've gone wrong with the boys, you probably would detonate the bomb immediately and Shiva would himself be dead. Shiva would never risk that — and tell me how did you put the vest on the boys without letting Shiva know?" Pa Jee is now visibly comfortable, as Uthman's words have given him an exit plan in case it is needed.

"Well, Pa Jee, it is not a bad question so I'll answer you, but that will be my last answer as I'm having to tell you the tricks of the trade here!"

"First of all, I did not hide from Shiva about the suicide vests on the boys. In fact, I made him check the vests himself and then connect them with the bombs on the speaker. He would have the remote so he will know that he is in control of the mission and no one else; not even the boys themselves and not even me. I also gave him another hundred thousand rupees to agree to this. In the worst case of the boys getting caught, he would use his gun and make a runner and we will give him cover. There was, however, one catch in this story. My engineer has programmed Shiva's remote with another one, which was with me, so if Shiva and the boys were to get caught, I would do the honours and create the explosion. Boom! All of them would die. But, of course, it did not come to that. The plan worked and, to be fair to Shiva, he executed it brilliantly!"

"So you managed to trick Shiva; lucky him he came out untouched! But, Uthman, you are a sly motherfucker! I wonder what you will do to me if shit ever hits the fan?" Pa Jee poses the question to Uthman without asking him directly.

"I will protect you to the very last, Pa Jee. You are special; you and I go back a long way and there is a common aim that we share — to destroy the Indians. Shiva was just a pawn motivated by money. Mine and your motivations are different — rather the same." Uthman smiles at Pa Jee, who gives him a broad smile back in return.

19

Kashif's early days at King's College are a breeze. As a foreign student, he had settled in London and the university incredibly swiftly. The main reason for this is because Kashif has left his residence with the boys back at Forest Gate and moved in with Hayley in her apartment in Bayswater with no rent to pay as Hayley wouldn't let him, considering his financial situation. He also doesn't have to worry about working long hours, so instead he can focus on his studies.

Kashif's Pakistani housemates in Forest Gate did not take his leaving well! They felt that they have been used by Kashif. So, they labelled him as selfish and insincere. Not having many close allies in a new country, Kashif felt more insecure and vulnerable. To counter that, he started to seek more and more solace in Hayley's company. He felt drawn to her by instinct — a man's desire to rest in the safest place akin to his mother's womb. Hayley's arms were a perfect haven. She looked after him well and Kashif repaid her by staying loyal to her.

Spooned next to each other one night after making love in the same position, Kashif felt the burden of his soul resting on Hayley's and, with a deep voice, he says, "I feel as if my soul rests with yours. I don't want to sound like a loser but isn't that what they call soul mates?"

Hayley laughs a short pleasing laugh, presses Kashif's hands tightly against her chest and then kisses his fingers. Kashif kisses her neck and holds her firmly. He wants to talk to her about their relationship — it is serious for him — he has found in her his future wife but he finds Hayley loving the moment and falling asleep. He feels like he would have to do the hard work of talking to her about this again some other time. He also doesn't want to break the blissful moment that he faces with Hayley. The quote of Gandhi keeps coming in his head — 'Speak only if it improves upon silence'. He becomes slightly apprehensive, concerned about the things to say and not scare Hayley off. 'Sometimes, to restart a conversation can be harder than the first time — but Hayley is no stranger', he says to himself!

Kashif finally plucks up some courage and says, "I hope you know that I am falling in love with you!"

With a big grin on her face, Hayley gives Kashif a passionate kiss and then says candidly, "That is because I am probably the first blonde that you've dated! Wait till it all wears out and other younger women chase after you in King's College. You'll be trying to get rid of me then!"

"Never in million years! It is not about the looks, Hayley. It is how I feel with you: like I've come home, I don't fear pain, I don't worry about any heart break, but I feel pure joy instead. And don't get me wrong — I wouldn't feel that way if you weren't this damn hot!" Now it is Kashif's turn to have a huge grin and he kisses Hayley back. His hand slides down to Hayley's butt, which is slightly cold; he squeezes her butt cheek with his warm hands.

Hayley stops kissing Kashif and says, with a concerned look in her eyes, "Don't get too attached, my love! I'm afraid that I'll break your heart! I must tell you something. I've got a four-year-old daughter who lives with her dad and her stepmother in Yorkshire. I go and visit her once a month and stay with my mom, so she gets to see her granny as well. I have a dog there too — he is a collie called Oscar. My daughter is called Sienna and my mom is Jess. They are both lovely and Sienna is the love of my life, of course. Because of my financial situation, or shall I say her dad is super rich, we decided it is best for Sienna to live with her dad. Her stepmother, Sharon, is good with kids — she has a two-year-old daughter who was one year old when she met my ex, George. Good thing is that we are all reasonably social with each other and Sienna and Sharon's daughter, Sophie, get along very well together, like sisters."

The look on Hayley's face changed from one of concern to happiness when she spoke about her daughter and the family. Kashif spotted that and kissed Hayley with even more passion. "That just makes you a yummy mummy and I've fallen for a MILF effectively! And all of this just makes me want you even more!"

Hayley smiles back and kisses him passionately, the tune *Promontory* from the movie *The Last of the Mohicans* comes up next on Hayley's playlist. She climbs on top of Kashif and they make love to the sound of the music in the background. Hayley moves back and forth effortlessly on Kashif with her hands planted on his chest while he has his placed lightly on either of her butt cheeks. Hayley cums first and then soon Kashif follows.

Lying next to each other, Kashif says to Hayley, "I have a confession to make as well, Hayley."

Hayley has a slightly concerned look on her face as she sees Kashif get out of bed and start searching for a notebook hidden inside his wardrobe.

"It might sound a bit, I don't know, like a loser to you but I write poetry." Hayley smiles back, moving her head sideways in disagreement. Kashif trawls through his diary. "Well, I am trying to find a poem which is not too personal — like about my first crush. Aha! There we go. This is something that I wrote against poaching of lions. It is actually a lion's point of view regarding modern day cowardly poaching versus older days... Would you like to listen to it?"

"Yes, my love!" Hayley places her palms underneath her face on the pillow and gives a glowing smile to Kashif, who reads to her while sat on the bed facing her.

Kings of their Realms
I do not confront them any more
Those masters of disguise
Day by day,
They grew wise
Thrilling were those days
When we exchanged stares
Sometimes they were more than us
Still there was nothing to fuss
For I knew who amongst them is the brave;
Not my flesh, but honor he would crave
I've once been captured by such a man
He let me be free so I understand
That pardon you can truly grant,

Only when you have the power to reprimand!
King of the Jungle I still remained
Wondering the fate of that man!
The eagle tells me the beasts surround him
Refusing to listen; cowardly denounce him
But he, the brave, would not succumb
Waiting patiently for his time to come
Says, "I have hunted all my life
Captured the best I could find
Once, every week or two
Stockpiling I did not do!"
As for the ones with the gun
I know they are here
It's their pungent smell
Hidden somewhere
My senses can tell,
How brave was he! As he dared
Fight me face to face so it is fair
But these gutless are hiding somewhere
Pity on them, for I am aware,
However, I will tread in the wild
Like a king shall!
Then there will be a deafening sound
Gradually I will fall to the ground
Glad not to have seen this cowardly beast
On a king's flesh the scoundrel will feast.
"I love you. I love this poem. You are amazing, my love."

Hayley gets up and kisses Kashif. Kashif puts his notebook aside and lies down facing the ceiling on his bed while Hayley goes down on him.

20

The dead bodies were lying around everywhere. The bodies of the boys have disintegrated into unrecognisable small pieces. Adnan's fake RADO watch is still on his left hand that is lying detached from his arm. Smooth Skin's face is not in one piece anymore; there is nothing left of the boys that one could recognise them from or even begin to construct what they looked like in flesh. What Uthman set out to execute, he did perfectly.

Browsing the news around the world while taking a little break from his coursework, Kashif comes across the news about the suicide bombing in Jammu & Kashmir. Looking upwards at the beautiful glass ceiling of the round reading room inside Maughan Library; Kashif begins to wonder whether there was any heaven or hell for the suicide bombers...

He imagines the fragmented body parts of the suicide bombers speaking out, 'We don't see the heaven that was promised to us when we were alive! Where is the Prophet who was meant to receive us as martyrs? Are we martyrs or are we just simply dead? Where are all those virgins? Is there even a life after death?

There is nothing present of the promises made to us by our leaders. We don't see or hear Allah! Is there an Allah like they speak of? Or has he also died with us? Neither there are the seventy-two virgins that were promised to us! No, not even a single one. We do not have any penis on us anymore to have sex with them!

Well then, is there a hell that will hold us and our leaders accountable for our atrocious deeds? And in that hell, we will receive the rightful punishment for our deeds? No, there isn't that either — we can't see it. Neither we nor our idea of the afterlife exist anymore.

The Quran says that on the judgement day, Allah will gather the dead from the dust and blow life in them again like he did in the first instance. Then, like everyone else, we will also be brought to justice. Who knows, we might well be pardoned then and maybe even honoured with the seventy-two virgins. Maybe we can partner up with the Prophet and ravage a few of those virgins together, one by one! Or we might just be condemned on the judgement day for killing other innocent life. Then we will be thrown into eternal fire and get bitten by nasty snakes. Maybe Allah will reward all the ones that were killed in the bomb blast by giving them the seventy-two virgins! Will there even be a judgment day?'

At this point Kashif takes a blue diary out from his ruck sack and starts writing...

'When the last bit of oxygen is consumed by the body parts then there must be nothing left of the suicide bombers; their souls must have died with them also. The plotters — the brains behind all this — are still at large and will be coming up with new schemes to cause havoc on God's earth.

And for the ones killed by the suicide bombers — their friends and families left behind will mourn them and will try to make sense of what had happened. The dead soldiers will be considered martyrs and assumed to have acquired a cosy place in a Hindu, Sikh or a Buddhist version of heaven or something similar. The suicide bombers will be considered villains if they ever get identified.

The families of the suicide bombers would never know what happened to their children. How their sons were turned into killers and their lives wasted for a cause which was probably never theirs. How they were groomed to die for a promise made to them by soulless manipulative men. They were encouraged to dream of a paradise as a resulting outcome of their suicidal actions. Actions commanded to them by their wicked leaders who themselves do not know any better about the life hereafter.

In this war there are no winners and no losers but only dead people. More and more every day, every hour, killed or killing for reasons that mean a lot to some but not much to the others. God does not speak with these wicked men anymore and neither does the devil. Even the devil is ashamed of their atrocities; it has stopped making its point to God — that man is unworthy. It is now clear to the devil that this God created man has transformed into a monster. The followers of these monster are weak; their will craves to be led by a will that is stronger than theirs and that is how they meet their destiny. God still speaks to its creation and perhaps also to human beings. Once he spoke of oneness and of creation and of life and love and humour — if only we humans had listened! The hell is here, the heaven is here, all here in the now. What will be tomorrow? For that, my guess is as good as yours.'

And then Kashif puts his pen down.